*Salisa Urenden's life* 🔖 **P9-AOS-044**

*standing still, going nowhere...*

"So that's what you want to tell your best friend the night before her wedding? That you're going to desert her again?" Before Salisa could answer, Ali tossed her head back and tucked her dark straight hair behind her right ear. "Well, that's fine," she said with an air of aloofness. "You missed us before. You realized how good you had it with Dale. You'll come back. Maybe by then you'll have come to your senses."

"You're right about why I'm going at least," Salisa began, trying to be bright and reassuring. "I just can't seem to get excited about life here any more.... In a few more years, we'll both be thirty, and you'll have your business, your husband, a house, and probably some kids. Everything you've always dreamed about! And I might still be sitting here not being able to say yes to Dale and not knowing why. So this seems like a good plan to me. I'll take a year off—and who can argue with my going on a mission trip?"

**Rena Eastman** is the pen name for Ronda Oosterhoff. She is a full-time editor for the David C. Cook Foundation. She also teaches piano to both children and adults "after my regular work." Besides her editorial work, she has written articles for inspirational periodicals. *Midsummer's Dream* is her first book for *Heartsong Presents*.

# Midsummer's Dream

*Rena Eastman*

*Heartsong Presents*

ISBN 1-55748-477-5

**MIDSUMMER'S DREAM**

PRINTED IN THE U.S.A.

# one

"Come into the kitchen with me," said Ali Lennox, pulling her resisting friend behind her. "I want to make sure I can get your thick hair into that new braid tomorrow."

"I still can't believe you want to be the hairdresser for your own wedding party," said Salisa Vrenden, waving an "I'll be back" sign to the group she left in the living room and then staying a step behind Ali down the short hallway that led to Ali's tiny kitchen.

Salisa took her place on her favorite stool—the one with the flashy red cushion—by the kitchen's island counter. "Okay, have at it, Ali. This will be the third time you've done it, but I know that this is your way of relieving stress."

Ali was already taking the braid out with a frenzy.

"Ow!" yelled Salisa, letting her head jerk back with Ali's yanks.

"Oh, quit exaggerating," said Ali. "It's my last night to do your hair as a beautician who's single. And I need to be with my maid of honor just now. I'm so nervous!"

Ali brushed and brushed, and then finally started twisting Salisa's shoulder-length, wavy, honey-blond hair. Salisa knew that sitting quietly for Ali was the best therapy she could offer her.

"I always told you it would look elegant pulled up, Sal," said Ali. "I'm so glad you let me talk you into growing it long. It's going to be absolutely perfect for tomorrow. Dale will be gazing at you the entire day."

"You're the bride, Ali," responded Salisa. "I would think that you would be worrying more about your looks than mine."

5

"But I do worry about you, Salisa. About you *and* Dale."

Salisa rolled her eyes. Whenever Ali brought Dale into a conversation more than once, Salisa knew what was coming.

"I've known for five years that I was going to marry Ted," said Ali, spinning Salisa around on the stool so that they faced each other. "And ever since you got back from college, it's always been the four of us—Ted and I and you and Dale. You've had the same five years with Dale, but you act like people get on your nerves when they even *hint* that *maybe* you should be thinking about marriage!"

"It does get on my nerves."

"Why?" Ali tilted her friend's face up so she could get a good look at the front of her hair. "What's so bad about the idea of marriage?" Ali's eyes searched Salisa's for an answer.

"Tell me the truth, Salisa," said Ali. Her look was so overly serious that Salisa had to stifle a giggle. "Do you want to be a nun?" This made both of them laugh, since double-dating and dreaming about men and marriage had been what had drawn them together in high school.

"Not at all," said Salisa, still chuckling. "I think it's great that you and Ted are fulfilling all your dreams. Your salon is all set up in the basement and your business is doing well. Now that Ted's done with pharmacy school . . . you're all set."

"And Dale has your dad's farm all paid off now, too," Ali reminded Salisa. "And you can't say that he hasn't worked hard at night school for that seminary degree you encouraged him to finish. So what are you waiting for? Your family's all here, you could have our beloved Reverend Rogers for a father-in-law, and you know you can have your job at the paper for as long as you want—unless, of course, you decide to have lots and lots of babies like me." Ali was grinning almost mischievously.

The thought of having babies and living next door to Ali all her life momentarily tempted Salisa. But something else tempted her more. "Ali," Salisa said, taking her friend's hands in hers. "Tomorrow is your wedding day. Think about the wonderful new adventure you're beginning. Don't think about me." Salisa's smile was genuine and warm.

But tears came to Ali's eyes. "That's just it, Salisa," she said, taking her hand to stop a sniffle. "We've always done everything together. Now I feel like we're heading off into two different directions." In a matter of seconds, Ali lapsed into her usual river of tears.

"You always were the first to cry," Salisa tried to joke. But her eyes were getting misty, too. *Poor Ali*, thought Salisa. *You don't know the half of it*. In addition to helping Ali through her prewedding jitters, Salisa was looking for a chance to tell her that their paths were diverging more than Ali suspected. *Ali's already a basketcase*, Salisa assessed. So she decided to plunge ahead.

"Here, Ali, have a seat," Salisa said, pulling Ali down onto the stool with the cornflower blue cushion. "This is just like old times. You and me." Then she jumped up to grab their usual Frescas from the refrigerator. Salisa popped them both open. "There," she said with compassion, pushing Ali's over in front of her.

"See?" said Salisa. "We'll always be able to do this. Your being married won't change that." She raised her can of Fresca for a toast and Ali obliged, smiling through her tears.

"Promise?" Ali asked. "Promise we'll always be like we are?"

Salisa weighed her words carefully. "Of course," she said. "As much as we can be."

Ali eyed her suspiciously. "What do you mean 'can?'"

"Well," Salisa began, evading Ali's direct glare, "as much as we can be. . .considering I'm going away for a short trip—just a short one, Ali."

"I knew it!" Ali jumped up, almost slamming her Fresca down on the counter. The tears started flowing again. "I could tell you had something like this up your sleeve."

Salisa tried to look innocent, but she knew she was in for another one of Ali's tirades.

"You're acting just like you did before you went on that three-month mission trip to Haiti," continued Ali. "You're restless. You mope whenever you're around Dale. He bothers you when he disagrees with you, and he bothers you more when he doesn't. You keep telling me you're bored in Pepperton and how you can't see yourself staying here forever, doing the same things day in, day out. I knew it!" Ali paced furiously, two steps to the refrigerator and two steps back.

"So that's what you want to tell your best friend the night before her wedding? That you're going to desert her again?" Before Salisa could answer, Ali tossed her head back and tucked her dark straight hair behind her right ear. "Well, that's fine," she said with an air of aloofness. "You missed us before. You realized how good you had it with Dale. You'll come back. Maybe by then you'll have come to your senses."

"You're right about why I'm going at least," Salisa began, trying to be bright and reassuring. "I just can't seem to get excited about life here anymore. And I guess your getting married has caused me to do something drastic."

"Me?" Ali gasped. "*I* cause *you* to do something drastic? Excuse me, but isn't it usually the other way around? You were always the one who instigated everything we did together. And I was always the one to get caught!"

For a few seconds, memories flashed through Salisa's mind: laundry detergent in the city fountain, toilet paper that "just happened" to go on local trees right before a rainstorm, and late-night escapes out windows after curfew. Salisa always had the ingenuity but Ali always got the blame.

Salisa could see that Ali was trying hard not to smile, so she kept going. "Ali," she said, pulling a well-worn letter from the pocket of her secondhand, oversized navy blazer. "Read this. You'll see. It's not so bad." Though she liked to dress casually, Salisa always managed to look somewhat chic, thanks to her classy ponytails and the dangling earrings Ali persuaded Salisa to wear.

Ali's eyes went back and forth down the letter as she read:

> *Thank you for applying to serve as a staff member for the Christian Union in England. In the past, American volunteers have contributed both spiritually and culturally to the academic life of our university communities, and we are looking forward to your being a part of that tradition. Below are the names of other volunteers who live near you with whom you may want to coordinate travel plans. The university you have been assigned to is listed next to your name. Please arrive no later than September 15.*

Ali looked up in alarm. "That's only three weeks away! Sal, how could you? My whole life is changing, and you're going to be halfway around the world!"

Salisa was relieved to see that her revelation was causing merely a blank look and not more tears. Ali had probably reached her emotional threshold for the day.

"Ali, look at it this way. I'm grieving, too. I feel like I'm losing you. In a few more years, we'll both be thirty, and you'll have your business, your husband, a house, and probably some kids. Everything you've always dreamed about! And I might still be sitting here not being able to say yes to Dale and not knowing why. So this seems like a good plan to me. I'll take a year off—and who can argue with my going on a mission trip?"

"Who said you weren't a part of my dreams?" Ali pointed out. "Life won't be the same in Pepperton without you."

Salisa poured what was left of her Fresca down the sink. "All I know is that I have to get out of the rut I'm in here," she said. "I'm not being fair to Dale, and I'm not being honest with anyone—including myself."

Ali was quiet for a moment. She didn't like being considered part of Salisa's "rut," but she knew her friend well enough not to argue with her plans. Then Ali's face lit up and Salisa could tell that Ali had thought of a sensible, not emotionally based, objection.

"How's your dad taking it?" Ali asked triumphantly. "You're not going to leave him all alone are you?"

Salisa had anticipated this from Ali. Both had lost their mothers to cancer and this, too, had drawn them close. "It's been over two years, Ali, and he's got to get on with his life. My being around only keeps him from learning to take care of himself. And a school year's not forever. It will just be long enough to train him." Salisa tried to laugh but couldn't.

Ali was deep in thought, trying to think of more reasons why Salisa should stay. She looked down at the letter again and skimmed through the dozen or so names and addresses.

"Hey! I know this person. Bennett Havana. And I think this Hazel Bright is his girlfriend. Ted knows Bennett from the hospital. I guess he's studying to be a some kind of surgeon. I wonder why he's going to England."

Salisa walked around the island to look at the name Ali was pointing to: Havana. The name sounded familiar. Then she remembered: A developer called Havana Associates was starting to take an interest in the farms just north of Pepperton. She had written an article about it for the local paper. It was only a matter of time before the urban creep of nearby Lansing would start to swallow the one-hundred-year-old Pepperton community.

Instantly, Salisa knew she would not like this Bennett Havana. While the slow pace of Pepperton sometimes threatened to suffocate her, she still felt a loyalty to the peaceful upbringing that had given her lifelong friends like Ali. Ted's friend was probably somewhat decent—at least he was going on a mission trip—but Salisa still distrusted his kind. She didn't think city people understood the importance of rural values.

Salisa continued to study the list. She and the two people Ali knew—Bennett and Hazel—were the only volunteers assigned to Abingdon University. She hadn't intended to point this connection out to Ali, but Ali noticed it anyway.

"Sal, it says here that they recommend people coordinate travel plans if they're going to the same place. I'll have Ted get Bennett's number and maybe you can travel with these two." Ali got up to find some paper. "I'd feel so much better if I knew you were safe. You know, it can get pretty dangerous in airports. I just heard on the news that—"

"Ali, I'm a grown woman! And besides, England's not an uncivilized country." She shook her head while Ali continued to write. "I'm sure I'll be fine."

But Ali had found something constructive to do about the situation. "Please go with someone, Sal. It's the least you can do. Please do it for me." Ali's big brown eyes were liquid with emotion.

"Okay," she quickly relented. "I guess it's the least I can do for a best friend that I'm deserting for a year."

Ali stood up and gave her friend a hug. "I'm never going to forgive you for springing this on me the night before my wedding," she said with a smile. "But if you promise to come back, I'll try to survive."

When Salisa didn't respond, Ali's brow furrowed. "You are coming back, aren't you?"

"Ali, all I know is that I have to go. I suppose Dale will come and get me if I don't decide to come back on my own.

You'll just have to trust that I know what I'm doing." Before Ali could get all emotional again, Salisa slid off her stool and put her arm in Ali's. "Let's go back in and see what the rest of your wedding party is up to. We've cried enough for one night, don't you think?"

The reminder that her guests were probably waiting for her in the living room spurred Ali on. "You're right. This is our night to celebrate!" She began to march out. "I can't wait to tell the others what you're going to do. Both of us are going to be leading such different lives."

"Ali, wait," Salisa said, holding her friend back. "Don't tell anyone yet—especially Dale. I'd rather leave quietly and let people talk about it when I'm gone. You know how this town is. People make a big deal out of everything."

"You've got to tell him as soon as you can," rebuked Ali. "He'll be crushed." She was used to trying to protect the soft-hearted Dale from Salisa's indifference.

"I know," Salisa whispered between gritted teeth. "But it has to be the right time. I'll tell him when there aren't so many people around."

"Poor Dale," Ali moaned softly as they rounded the corner of the hallway.

Most of Ali's guests were engrossed in a board game in the middle of the room. But Ted, Ali's soon-to-be husband, looked up and gave a heart-melting smile to his bride-to-be. *These two are really in love,* thought Salisa. *I can't imagine what they must be feeling.*

"Where'd you go?" An eager, six-foot, four-inch man lumbered his way up to Salisa. "I suppose you two were having your last night of girl talk." Dale Rogers laughed as if he had said something funny.

"Actually, you're right," Salisa smiled toward him. "We always have good talks, don't we, Ali?" But Ali was already across the room, sitting on Ted's lap.

"Any chance you're going to fill me in?" asked Dale.

"Whenever you two get all gooey-eyed, I know you're up to something."

Salisa wanted to be kind to Dale, but something about his beaming face made her want to run in the other direction. Ali must have noticed Salisa's discomfort, for she quickly came back over. Salisa thought Ali was going to get Dale involved with the board game, but instead Ali smiled sweetly and said, "Why don't you two go take a walk outside?" Dale needed no further cajoling. "We've finished fixing up the yard," Ali continued, "and we've made a path that links the two side roads. It's a beautiful walk through the bean fields at night."

"Great idea, Ali!" exclaimed Dale.

Salisa glared at her friend. Ali had backed her into a corner—with Dale.

"I suppose I'll need a jacket then," said Salisa, turning to walk toward the closet. "It might get chilly out there." Salisa looked back and saw Ali whispering to Dale. By his expressions, Salisa knew that Ali was inadvertently getting his hopes up. . .as usual.

"I'm sure Salisa will tell you all about it," Ali was saying when Salisa returned.

Dale's nodding told Salisa he couldn't wait.

"I suppose I'll have to now," said Salisa, walking up to them. "C'mon, Dale. Let's go check out those beans."

## two

"Wake up! Wake up, Salisa!"

Salisa jumped a little when she saw the face of a green-eyed, bushy-haired man looking down at her. She tried to get a better look, but her heavy eyelids slid back down. Never had she been this tired before. She turned her head to the right and noticed that trees were flying past her. Gray trees. No, green trees on a gray background. *I'm on the train*, she finally remembered. The six-hour time difference between America and England had given Salisa a full-blown case of jet lag.

"What time is it?" Salisa asked turning her head back toward the curly-haired man who had introduced himself as Bennett Havana at the start of their journey.

"Three-thirty," Bennett replied with talk show pizazz. He smiled widely, revealing deep dimples. His hair, Salisa surmised, probably looked nice when it was clean and combed, but it looked rather wild as a result of the day's travel. The woman sitting next to him, Hazel, showed none of the typical signs of grubbiness. She obviously had recently applied her thick magenta lipstick and her dark, sleek hair was pulled back into a designer barrette.

"We'll be there in a half an hour," the exuberant Bennett announced. He smiled again, this time with greater energy.

Hazel looked up from her travel guide and gazed at him. "It's going to be so romantic," she whispered, her lips over-emphasizing the words.

Hazel's cooing irritated Salisa. In fact, everything about Hazel irritated Salisa. Hazel was the exact opposite of what Salisa enjoyed about Ali. Both were glamorous in a dark,

14

exotic kind of way, but while Ali's beauty was natural and seemed to fit her emotional, sometimes zany behavior, Hazel's appeared artificial. Salisa knew she was being judgmental, but she had no interest in getting to know Hazel better, therefore proving her instincts right or wrong.

But Bennett had other ideas. Now that Salisa was finally awake, he was eager to get a three-way conversation going.

"Did you have a good nap?" he began, almost visibly bouncing. He easily filled the seat across the small table between them and, in his bright red flannel shirt and faded jeans, he reminded Salisa of a lumberjack. *He hardly looks or acts like he's part of a suburban real estate family*, thought Salisa, *which is just as well*. She nodded a silent yes to his question about her nap.

"I was hoping we'd get a chance to talk before we arrived in Abingdon," Bennett tried again. This full-grown man was clearly excited. When Salisa didn't respond immediately, Bennett came up with, "So, we both know Ted Stromley."

Salisa glanced at Hazel who was intently filing her nails. Resigning herself to the fact that Bennett wanted to talk to her, she sat up and pushed some of her hair away from her face. Travel dirt was making it clumpish and wavier than usual.

"Yes, Ted's a great guy," Salisa began. "He makes friends wherever he goes." Salisa felt a yawn coming and put her hand over her mouth as she tipped her head back. Maybe if she looked tired enough, Bennett would leave her alone.

"How'd he meet his wife—Ali?" Bennett asked. "You two are friends, right?"

Salisa decided she might as well be civil. She would give him the basics. She sighed, trying to show that her answer required effort. "Ted grew up about a half-hour away from Pepperton, where Ali and I grew up, and his church and our church have these singles' get-togethers. Boy meets girl and

five years later, they marry." Salisa hoped this would sat-
isfy Bennett.

But the topic only drew Hazel into the conversation. She
looked over at Bennett. "It was simply destiny for us, wasn't
it, dear?" Hazel's voice was soft and smooth.

"I'd like to think there's a little bit more to it than that,"
replied Bennett as he turned to look at his admiring partner.

"It was simply meant to be," Hazel said, finally acknowl-
edging Salisa. Her huge, blue, perfectly lined eyes were
round with expression. "I was taking my third graders—
they're complete beasts—out for a walk to the park, and
Bennett happened to be at an outdoor ceremony getting an
award for professional excellence."

Bennett was shaking his head, but he was still smiling.
"How many times do I have to tell you, Hazel?" He tweaked
her cheek. "The award was simply for community service."
He looked back at Salisa. "I like to help out at the clinic for
low-income families," he explained. "It's a really nice
facility. Do you get into Lansing often, Salisa? The clinic
isn't far—"

"Bennett, honey, I doubt that Salisa is interested in visiting that place. What's important is that nice people like you
work there. But you won't have to once your residency is
done." She leaned over and gave him a peck on the cheek,
leaving a lip print. "I can't wait until you're a real doctor!"

Bennett instinctively wiped the lip print off. He was still
smiling, but Salisa thought there was a tinge of wooden-
ness about it. Calmly, he turned to Hazel.

"I don't work there because I have to," he said in a hushed
voice. "I've told you over and over that I like it. I like to
help people. I think my clinic work is something God wants
me to do."

Hazel got noticeably uncomfortable and giggled nervously
as she looked back at Salisa.

"Bennett is quite fervent about his faith. And, of course, I am too. We just express it differently. And," Hazel went on, her voice increasing in volume, "this year is supposed to be some kind of faith test for us, right, Bennett? Isn't that how you described it?" Hazel's well-powdered face flashed a conniving look that quickly turned back into her cool smile.

Bennett was unperturbed. "It's important that people have the same goals in mind," he explained to Salisa. "When I told Hazel I wanted to do this for a year, she said she wanted to go, too. I didn't make her come along. This kind of work shouldn't be jumped into lightly. . .or for the wrong reasons."

"I completely agree," said Hazel, who was briskly buffing her nails. Then, both Bennett and Hazel happened to look at Salisa.

"Of course," added Salisa quickly. "I completely agree with both of you . . . too. People shouldn't do mission work for the wrong reasons." She shook her head with what she hoped looked like sincere dismay. A glance at Bennett, however, revealed that he had caught her hesitation.

"I'm sure we'll have more time to talk about all this once we're settled into our work at Abingdon," said Bennett. Salisa watched a twinkle come into his eyes as they caught sight of something out the window. "But for the moment, I think both of you should take a look at the magnificent cathedral coming into view. Ladies, we're in Abingdon!"

# three

The train slowed and circled what looked like a small town. Out of the center of it rose the most majestic, ancient looking church Salisa had ever seen. Within a few moments, the train had slipped into the town and they lost sight of the cathedral.

The train soon stopped and passengers stood up and collected their luggage. Bennett dutifully rounded up Hazel's leather-and-flower-stitched bags, also grabbing Salisa's sturdy Samsonite just before she reached for it.

"Thanks, Bennett," said Salisa. "You don't have to do that."

"No problem," he replied, still wearing his eternal grin.

"No, really, I can get it," Salisa said firmly, taking her large suitcase from him. "You have enough to carry as it is." Salisa glanced at Hazel who was carrying her pretty toiletry bag and not much else.

The three of them began shuffling their luggage down the platform's high steps. "How are we going to get all of this to our rooms?" Hazel whined. "And how do we know where to go?"

Bennett scanned the people on the platform. Salisa watched his face break into a look of relief. He pointed. "There she is. Our contact." A short, stout woman with a black coat and scarf stood off to one side, waiting expectantly for someone. She held a small sign with the letters CU scribbled in black marker.

"What's a CU?" asked Hazel.

"It stands for Christian Union," replied Salisa as pleasantly as she could. "Our jobs for the year." Hazel must not have read the literature from England very closely and Hazel probably didn't know also that she would be called a "rep," which stood for "postgraduate Christian Union representative."

The lady in black had seen Bennett's wave of recognition and ambled up to them. "You must be the CU staff members from America," she said, not waiting for an answer before she started helping them with their luggage.

"We sure are," Bennett said heartily.

*Why is he always so perky?* Salisa wondered. While she was glad Bennett wasn't as sour as Hazel, she was looking forward to that evening when she would be alone and wouldn't have to deal with either one of their personality extremes.

"Just come this way and I'll have you dropped off at your colleges." The woman directed them to a small minibus. They took turns piling themselves and their luggage onto its narrow seats, with Hazel insisting hers not be "smooshed at the bottom."

"To Chadwick College," the lady in black told the driver. The minibus lurched forward and began descending a steep hill that turned round and round the base of the train station.

The woman started rummaging around in her satchel. "By the way, I'm Maureen. I'm the international student coordinator. You are . . .?" She was scanning the list she had just pulled out. "Bennett Havana?" Maureen pulled her glasses down with her one free hand and made eye contact with Bennett.

"That's right," Bennett answered with his characteristic enthusiasm.

Salisa was beginning to understand why Bennett and Ted Stromley got along so well. Both had the same strain of cheerfulness running through every word and action.

"Good," Maureen continued. "And who is . . . Hazel?"

Maureen looked up at Salisa first, but then Hazel said, "I am." Hazel blinked her eyes demurely.

"Then you must be Salisa." Maureen turned toward Salisa.

"Yup," Salisa replied, immediately regretting it. Why did she always have to betray her farm background by her silly rural slang? Oh, well. This was to be her year of freedom, spiritual growth, and cultural refinement.

As Maureen wrote a few notes on her papers, the minibus pulled up to a small stone building that looked like an overgrown cottage.

"Here we are," Maureen called out in a singsong voice. "Ian, please help these two unload their luggage. Bennett Havana and Hazel Bright will be lodging at Chadwick College." Maureen put two brisk checkmarks on the piece of paper in her hand.

Salisa looked at Bennett and Hazel as they prepared to get off the minibus. "I guess this is it," she said cheerfully. "I'll see you around."

"Goodbye, Salisa," said Hazel.

"Yes, goodbye," echoed Bennett, shaking Salisa's hand vigorously. "Take care. It was great traveling with you. We'll get your number and give you a call or something."

"You did know that there aren't any phones in individual rooms, didn't you?" interjected Maureen. "You'll have to use the public ones in the lobbies of each of the colleges and hope that people take messages for you."

"That will be fine," said Salisa. "I'm sure we'll manage."

Bennett stopped and looked puzzled for a moment, but then he quickly realized Hazel was already off the minibus and waiting for him.

"We'll find each other," he said, turning toward Salisa one last time. "This place can't be that confusing." And, with one last incredibly rich smile, he was gone.

Finally, Salisa was alone. The minibus pulled away and soon began rambling through winding streets, jostling her as it went over roads that felt like they were just piles of rocks.

"We're taking you to St. Anne's, where you'll be staying," Maureen announced, gathering her long skirt around her ankles and turning in her seat so she could face Salisa more directly. "It has a lovely setting, although it's always hard to get the full effect when one is dealing with British weather."

"I *did* notice how gray it is here," said Salisa, understating the obvious. "But I kind of like the moistness." The damp air and misty rain had refreshed Salisa. While Ali had thought the weather would be the worst part of Salisa's time in England, Salisa had actually looked forward to it. Cloudy weather always made her feel more alive, more creative, and more bookish. She always got more done when it was raining.

"Maureen," Salisa ventured after a few seconds of silence. "I noticed that you don't have a British accent. Are you from America?"

"Actually, yes." Maureen grew animated. "I married my British husband when he was studying American History in Washington, D.C." She smiled at the memory. "I knew that moving here was a part of the deal when I accepted his proposal and I have never regretted my decision."

"No?" Salisa was intrigued. Marrying a British man sounded like a great way to escape the routine of everyday life back home.

Then she saw it. The gray stone building looked like something from an old black-and-white movie—a haunted house with clouds that were moving too fast behind its peaked towers. The front of the building had wide steps leading up to a central entrance, and two wide wings of bleak windows stretched out to either side. The highest windows seemed to emanate darkness rather than allow light in. Salisa shuddered. Her fears were realized when Maureen chirped,

"Here we are! I hope you like it."

As Maureen helped Salisa unload her bags, Salisa began to wonder how she and her travel companions had ended up with such different-looking residences. Salisa ventured, "Maureen, can you tell me once more how the 'college system' works here? I'm still not sure I understand it."

"Gladly," said Maureen, although it was clear that she didn't have much time for small talk. "Abingdon has thirteen colleges, such as Chadwick and St. Anne's, each of which has its own dining hall, social clubs, sport teams, and, of course, CU, where you'll be working. And, as you can probably tell by the two you've seen, each college has a distinct personality. Most students stick pretty closely to their college, but there is some mingling, especially for a college like St. Anne's, which is all girls."

"But some of the colleges house both men and women, right?"

"Exactly. Actually, St. Anne's is the only single-sex college left. Durbyfield was the last to be all-male, but it's going mixed this year. With that, every college but St. Anne's will be mixed. The headmistress prefers it that way. And, speaking of her highness," said Maureen almost flippantly, "there she is." Maureen tipped her head toward the tall, thin woman walking toward them.

"Salisa," continued Maureen, gasping because she was finding Salisa's luggage heavier than she had expected, "this is Judith Pendrill. Judith, here's your American."

"Welcome," Miss Pendrill said smoothly, clasping Salisa's hand with strong formality. "We're *so* glad to have you with us. Welcome to St. Anne's."

Salisa glanced down at the headmistress's hands, trying not to be obvious. *Of course*, she acknowledged. *This place is for spinsters!* But that was just as well. Making a decision about Dale was foremost in Salisa's mind and her conscience wouldn't let her pursue anything else while the issue was still unresolved.

"I'll let you two get acquainted," said Maureen, leaving Salisa's luggage on the front stone steps. "If you need me, Salisa, I'm in my office in the mornings. It's in Wiltshire Hall on Gates Street." Maureen nodded to Miss Pendrill and then hoisted herself back up into the minibus.

Turning to Miss Pendrill, Salisa was immediately unnerved by her gaunt, gray face. Close-up, her eyes were large and glassy and her lips were paper thin.

"I'll show you to your room," the teeth said, and Salisa realized she was staring. Salisa followed Miss Pendrill up the stone steps, into a hallway with tall ceilings, and then toward a white, wooden, rickety staircase.

Miss Pendrill climbed smoothly, without moving her head. "Did Maureen give you any details about an orientation schedule?" She let the walls of the staircase reflect her words back toward Salisa.

"Not really," said Salisa, following her. "But I did receive quite a bit of information in the mail before I left about the college CU's. So I've been studying that."

"I see," said Miss Pendrill, opening the door to what must have been Salisa's floor. "It's a good thing I take some of these matters into my own hands," Miss Pendrill muttered to herself but loud enough for Salisa to hear.

The corridor where they emerged was dark and lifeless. When they reached one of the last doors on the left, Miss Pendrill announced, "This is it. Room 214." Then, with weary eyes, she turned to look at Salisa. "I've asked Sophie Barnes to watch out for you. She was in your position last year, and she's staying on to serve as a CU senior adviser and to direct the university's Shakespeare Society. Her room is at the end of this hall," Miss Pendrill stopped to point, "and she'll be expecting a visit from you." Then, Miss Pendrill grew stern. "I hope  you'll take advantage of the arrangements I've made for you, Miss Vrenden."

With that, Miss Pendrill excused herself to finish some work. Salisa heard her flat heels echo down the linoleum stairway.

Salisa unlocked her door and let it swing open on its own. Her dingy newspaper office back home suddenly seemed warm and inviting. Here, the walls were a pasty turquoise, a *peeling* pasty turquoise at that. The bed had a mattress that looked about as thick as the kind in a baby's crib. One flimsy sheet and a rough army-type blanket covered the bed, and the pillow the college had provided was covered with coffee-colored, rose-shaped stains. Her "washbasin"—every college room in Britain had one—appeared okay. Aside from the old faucets that would channel scalding water on one side and freezing cold on the other, it would do. A lone, naked light bulb hung above her, and a small, flat, flannel rug covered a few square feet of the cold floor.

Salisa began unpacking and waited for the thrill of independence to overtake her. She had waited months for this moment! But something wasn't right. It wasn't as exciting as Salisa had hoped. And the crumbly corners seemed to suck up any warmth or cheeriness Salisa tried to bring to her new home.

*If only I could make a quick phone call*, Salisa thought. *Then I could get past this initial "settling in" time.* But what would Ali think of her calling so soon? Salisa listened to the wind as it spattered droplets on her small window.

Despite her attempt to will them away, the tears started falling, dripping hot, salty wetness onto her cheeks. What if this year turned out to be difficult and trying? Would it be because God hadn't wanted her to come in the first place? What if He really did want her to stay in Pepperton and live on a farm and be a pastor's wife?

Slowly, Salisa pushed her empty suitcase under the bed and rolled up her sweatshirts to use as a pillow. *I always like falling asleep to the sound of rain*, Salisa reminded herself. But somehow the sound didn't comfort her here.

In her last few moments of consciousness, Salisa prayed to God that she would wake up loving her new life and not missing what she had left at home. Her mind began to drift toward scenes of walks with Dale and talks with Ali, but the musty smell of her blanket kept reminding Salisa she was alone in a dark, damp, spooky-looking college.

The taste of freedom was starting to turn just a little sour.

# *four*

"I think that Miss Pendrill has me on a wild goose chase!" Salisa exclaimed to Maureen later that week. "I don't think this Sophie is a real person. It looks like someone's been reading the notes I leave, but then I never see anyone. I've tried for days to find her."

"Judith's always taking things way too seriously," laughed Maureen, pouring Salisa a cup of coffee from a dirty coffeepot in her crowded attic office. "You'll do fine with or without Sophie Barnes. I've met her. She's a charming young woman, but she is hard to catch up with."

"So what do I do in the meantime?" Salisa asked. "I've been here for almost a week now, and I'm not getting as involved as I'd like to be."

"Whoa," said Maureen, gesturing for emphasis and forgetting that she still had coffee in her cup. "I should know by now that most Americans who end up in Abingdon are the driven, exploratory, and serious type—much different from the Brits who know how to enjoy life with a nice, slow cup of tea. I'm finally learning," she said, tipping her cup up to her mouth, "but I still prefer coffee." She finished hers off.

"You have only a few more free days left, Salisa," said Maureen, getting up to refill her cup. "The first term starts Monday. After that, the pace picks up. So, if I were you, I'd try to enjoy the extra time."

"I have been," Salisa protested. "I've wandered all through town and into the countryside some, but it's kind of hard to enjoy walking when it keeps raining all the time."

Maureen chuckled. "You seem like the sort who is going

to need a little bit more than sunshine and the CU to keep her satisfactorily occupied. Would you say that's true, Salisa?"

"I can't say for sure, Maureen," said Salisa, "since I don't know what Abingdon is like with either of those—sun or students. But I do know that I'm the type who likes to have more than one thing going on. For example, at home, I write and edit at the local newspaper. But that's not my life. I play the piano at church, and I tutor a few students a week in English literature and composition—that's what I studied in college."

Maureen set her coffee cup down so she could clap her hands together. "Then I know just the thing!" Maureen's reaction piqued Salisa's curiosity. "The English department has been asking me to keep an eye out for an American who could volunteer time as a writing tutor. They like the way Americans are taught how to structure an essay, so they're looking for someone to tutor a few British students. Does that kind of work interest you?"

Salisa's face had lit up at the words "writing tutor." Her Tuesday tutoring sessions back home had been the highlight of her week.

"That sounds perfect!"

Maureen was pleased with the match she'd made. But then Salisa grew solemn. "Won't people like Miss Pendrill think I'm neglecting my CU duties?"

"My experience with Americans," answered Maureen, "has been that most of them have more interests and energy than they know what to do with. And as for Judith, I can't imagine that she would argue with the idea of getting more mileage out of one of our international students!"

"So I have the job?"

"You have the job," Maureen smiled. "You'll have a small office in the English department building with a sign-up sheet on your door. Students will be able to make appointments with you when they need them." She poured herself another cup of coffee and took a good look at Salisa. "I had a feeling when I picked you up at the station, Salisa, that you were game for a full-course English experience."

"I am," said Salisa. "And I appreciate your help in getting me started."

"Any time," said Maureen. "I just have one word of caution."

"What's that?"

"The English experience is addictive," said Maureen. "I'm still living mine, and I wouldn't be surprised if someone like you gets addicted as well."

## five

The short, lively woman running through the dining hall had to be Sophie. She looked slightly older than the rest of the students and her raven black pageboy bounced as she nodded and waved.

"Sophie!" Salisa tried calling. Sure enough, the woman looked her way but, not seeing anyone she recognized, she turned and resumed spooning bran flakes into her bowl. Salisa waited for her to sit down and then ventured over.

"Sophie Barnes?"

The woman looked up. Then her face broke into a grin and she stood, almost knocking the bench over behind her. She pumped Salisa's hand enthusiastically.

"Salisa Vrenden! I recognize your accent. I'm ever so sorry we haven't met up yet. I've been comin' to your door nearly every mornin' but you're always already gone! I guess you must be running late today?"

Salisa smiled. "Actually I'm just taking it easy since I hear that everything goes crazy once the term starts."

"You got that right," said Sophie, between bites of cereal. "Here, sit yourself down. We've got a few minutes to chat anyway. Could you come 'round for tea tonight—say ten o'clock?" Sophie's singsong British accent had so captured Salisa's attention that she had almost missed what Sophie was saying.

"I'm ever so sorry I've been hard to catch and that tea will have to wait until then," Sophie kept chattering, "but I promise I'll be there."

"If not, just leave a note that tells me when to come back," said Salisa.

"I'm not much for notes—as you probably figured out by now," said Sophie. Sophie ate a few spoonfuls of cereal and then she tipped her bowl toward her chin and sipped the rest of the milk. "I've gotta run," she said, excusing herself. "But I'm walking down to the English building. Care to join me? It'll be a fast walk, but we can chat on the way."

"Sure," said Salisa, jumping up to keep pace with Sophie. She had wanted to go scout out her new tutoring office anyway. "Do I have time to run upstairs to brush my teeth?"

"You Americans are all alike!" said Sophie with amazement. "I knew one last year who did the same thing—always washin' and fussin' and brushin' her teeth. Well, then, hurry up. I might as well wait, now that you've found me."

Salisa ran up the stairs, two at a time. She had hardly had the toothpaste on her toothbrush when she heard a tap at her door.

"Hurry up, Salisa! It's me, Sophie. It's time we're headin' down."

Salisa's teeth would have to wait. She grabbed her jacket and backpack and followed Sophie into the hallway, almost catching her jacket in the doorway. She had to nearly bound down the stairs to keep up with Sophie, but fortunately Sophie paused outside the front entrance of St. Anne's, allowing Salisa to zip her backpack and do a quick check to see if she was prepared to spend most of the day in town.

"Ah, smell that country air," said Sophie, gulping in deep breaths. "And there's not a view like this in all of northern England!" St. Anne's was perched on a hill that overlooked the oldest part of Abingdon and rising up from the very center of town was the majestic Abingdon Cathedral.

As they stood there, the slightest bit of sunlight began to peek through the clouds. Sophie tipped her head back and closed her eyes, waiting for a faint bit of warmth on her face.

"Isn't it a great day to be alive?" she breathed.

"It sure is," agreed Salisa, again letting a rural twang slip out but sensing that it amused and interested Sophie. "When the air's clear and bright like this," Salisa went on to observe, "the cathedral looks close enough to touch."

"Well," said Sophie, setting out, "I know all the best vantage points 'round here. I'll show them to you sometime if you want."

"I'd love that," said Salisa. But she doubted that she'd be able to keep up with Sophie long enough to follow her anywhere. Though Salisa's gait was longer, Sophie's little legs moved so fast that Salisa had to almost run to catch up with her. They went down a small gravel path, crossed the main road near a roundabout—Britain's solution for intersections—and then walked and slid down a slippery, wooded bank toward the Dell River.

"Sophie, this is beautiful!" Salisa exclaimed when they reached a clearing that led to a wide, stone bridge. "Nobody told me these paths were here."

Sophie ran ahead and planted herself in one of the bridge's side balconies. The small platforms had enough room for several people to step up and over the water, against a stone guardrail, away from the main traveling path of the bridge.

"This is Mill Bend Bridge," announced Sophie, turning briefly to look at Salisa. Then her voice took on a dreamlike quality and she cooed, "Ah, isn't it lovely?" Sophie closed her eyes and began waving her arms back and forth over the river. An old mill was on the right-hand bank and the twin towers of the cathedral's west end towered over the banks above the mill. The sun was growing visibly warmer and stronger.

Salisa joined Sophie on the small ledge. The smell of wet, fresh air gave Salisa a tinge of spring fever, even though it was autumn. Salisa began to close her eyes but quickly opened them when she felt movement next to her. Sophie was off again.

"Tell me about the Shakespeare Society," Salisa called out ahead of her, realizing that if they were going to have any real conversation on this journey, she would have to start it.

Sophie slowed to talk with her. Her animated face told Salisa that this topic was the way to her heart. "As an undergraduate," Sophie quickly began, "I had parts in *Julius Caesar, Much Ado about Nothing,* and *The Taming of the Shrew.* Then last year, I was stage manager for *Romeo and Juliet.* This year I'm directing *A Midsummer Night's Dream.*" Sophie stopped walking to do a little jig. "That's what I've been working on these last few days—getting everything set up for the auditions, stage assignments, and all that."

Salisa's mind was churning fast. It didn't sound like spending time with the rookie CU rep was a high priority for Sophie. How was she going to learn the ins and outs of St. Anne's CU if Sophie was always working on her play?

Salisa had an idea. "Sophie," she began, "do you by any chance need an assistant? You know, the kind of person who sits with you at rehearsals, runs errands with you . . . that kind of thing."

Salisa might have imagined it, but it seemed as if Sophie visibly slowed her pace even more than when they had started talking about Shakespeare, and then she turned to study Salisa.

"I've always wanted to be part of a Shakespearean production," Salisa went on enthusiastically. "I studied all his works in college, but I never got to be part of an actual performance group."

Sophie stopped in the middle of the footpath. "Do you know his plays well?" she asked cautiously.

"For an American I do," said Salisa. "I liked my year-long Shakespeare class so well in college that I did my nior project on the Early Plays. I know *Romeo and Juliet* he best," Salisa admitted. "But you already did that last ear. Too bad I had to miss out on the world's greatest omance."

"Then consider yourself appointed," said Sophie, almost reaking into a run again. "And, as for *Romeo and Juliet* eing Shakespeare's greatest romance, that's rubbish! So aany people think that's Shakespeare's one and only play. happen to think that *A Midsummer Night's Dream* is by far he most romantic play Shakespeare ever wrote." Sophie alked faster as the volume of her voice increased. "The ombination of its silliness and its other-worldliness makes the perfect mirror of reality. I can't wait to get workin' on !" In her excitement, she clapped a few times and then ut her arm through Salisa's. "And I can't wait to put my ssistant to good use."

"Keep in mind," Salisa reminded her, "that my main job ere is the CU. And I've already signed up to be a tutor in he English building for a few hours in the mornings."

"Don't worry about that," said Sophie. "I think you've it upon a marvelous idea. You can help me with the play nd I'll help you with CU ideas. And," Sophie continued, caling a steep part of the bank and pulling Salisa behind er, "the Shakespeare Society will be a good way to get to now students outside St. Anne's. I didn't do enough of that ast year."

Salisa hadn't thought about this before, but it was a good oint. Her tutoring would help in this respect, too.

"It's settled then," continued Sophie, as if she was afraid alisa would reconsider. "You can't back out now."

"Why not?"

"Who knows when else you'll be able to catch me?" ophie displayed a mischievous smile.

"I'll see you tonight," Salisa reminded her. "You promsed!"

"Oh, all right," replied Sophie. The path they were on suddenly emerged between two buildings, one of which was the English building. They entered it, and Sophie turned down the hall that led to the theater. "When you come tonight," she turned around as if suddenly remembering something, "bring your pictures."

Salisa gave her a blank look.

"Just bring 'em," Sophie replied, resuming her walk away from Salisa. "Americans always have 'em and when you ask Americans to show 'em to you, they always have loads of good stories to tell."

*That means I'll have to tell her all about home,* Salisa thought. *And just when I was beginning to feel captured by this wonderful new culture!*

Despite Salisa's doubt that Sophie would actually be in her room that night, she walked over. Sophie's door was open a few inches, and light and the smell of toasted cheese was coming from Sophie's room.

"Salisa? Is that you?" a voice from inside called. "I can see your shadow. Come on in."

Salisa pushed the door inward and saw Sophie sitting Indian style on her orange carpet, buttering both sides of a flat sandwich.

"You haven't had late-night toasties here in England yet, have you?" Sophie asked, looking up with a grin. "Americans usually don't even have a teakettle, let alone a toastie maker. Here, have a seat." Sophie scattered a few clothes toward the corners of the room, making room for Salisa to sit down next to her. Sophie's room was larger than Salisa's and, because it was a suite, it had an extra bed in it. But both beds were covered with at least ten inches of what looked like Elizabethan costumes.

"They're for the play," said Sophie, noticing Salisa's glances between the two piles. "We're already trying things on and sending them out for alterations."

"So it's going well so far?" asked Salisa, joining her friend on the floor. "When do you want me to start helping out?"

"Well, you can start by coming to the primary rehearsals that are weekdays from three-thirty in the afternoon until five-thirty or so. How does that sound?"

"Great," said Salisa, taking a toasted cheese—"toastie"—from Sophie.

"But we're not here to talk about the play," said Sophie, scooting her toastie maker away so she could face Salisa on what little floor space was available. "You're here to show me your pictures and to tell me all about your life in America."

Although Salisa hadn't thought she was in the mood for chatty company that night, she warmed up to Sophie as soon as she saw that Sophie was genuinely interested in what her life was like back home. Sophie asked an average of five questions per picture, some of which Salisa didn't mind answering—and some of which she did.

"You almost married this man? What did you say his name was—Dale?"

Hearing someone else say his name brought a rush of unexpected memories. "Um, yes," Salisa said softly. "Well, no, I didn't almost marry him. It's just that the issue came up more than once. . .and with increasing frequency over the last year or so."

"And this is your best friend. . .the one in the weddin' dress?"

"Yes. That's Ali." Why did seeing the photos again bring back such strange emotions? Ali looked content and happy, and Salisa couldn't decide whether she missed the comfort of their relationship or was enjoying her separate identity.

"So, do you miss them?" asked Sophie, as if reading Salisa's thoughts. Sophie started her second round through the pile of pictures. "I would think you would. Everyone looks like they get on well with each other."

"I do and I don't," Salisa answered truthfully. "On one hand, seeing all these pictures makes me wonder what prompted me to plop myself in England for a year. But on the other hand, the time away seems good and right and natural. . .the perfect thing for me to do right now."

"But where does that leave you with your friends back home. . .especially this Dale? What will happen while you're gone?"

Salisa was quiet for a moment. "We left it that this year would be the deciding point for us. Dale thinks the time away will be what I need in order to be able to accept his proposal."

"And you?"

"All I know is that this year will help me decide."

"Whether or not to marry him?"

"That's what I'm thinking."

"But what if you decide you don't want to marry him while you're here? Won't it be difficult to go back then?"

Salisa pulled her knees up to her chin. "Actually, I haven't allowed myself to think about that possibility," she finally said. "That'd be tough. Anyway, I have almost a whole year to sort things through. I'm just depending on God to give me some kind of answer by then."

"Sometimes He has us do the dirty work, not Him," Sophie said gently.

"I don't understand."

"I'm just speakin' from experience," said Sophie, gathering up the pictures and sliding them back into the processing envelope in which Salisa had brought them over. "Sometimes we like to delegate to God the choices He wants us to make ourselves."

"Are you saying that this is something I shouldn't consult God about?"

"On the contrary," said Sophie, getting up. "You need to

put Him first in all your decisions. All I'm sayin' is that it sounds like you may know more than you think you know, and maybe you're just waitin' for a way to use Him as an excuse."

"That's not true!" cried Salisa, rising up to meet Sophie face to face. "I really don't know what I want, and that's why I'm here."

"Okay, okay," said Sophie, trying to soothe Salisa. "I'm not trying to pick a fight. Just forget I said anything. We're supposed to be getting together to talk about St. Anne's CU, and the last thing we need is arguments about this kind of thing."

"I agree," said Salisa with an edge in her voice. "So let's not bring it up again. This is my year away from America— and American people."

"You can't. . .," Sophie began, then thought otherwise. "Here," she said, bringing a more upbeat tone to their conversation. She turned to one of her overcrowded bookshelves and pulled out a well-worn binder with differently colored, loose sheets of paper sticking out from it. "This is my CU notebook from last year. It's full of schedules, Bible study outlines, announcements. . .that kind of thing." She was already flipping the pages. "Let's start by going through this."

Sophie and Salisa spent the next hour and a half sipping tea, munching on second toasties, and building each other's excitement for what the year might bring. Sophie wisely forgot to bring up America again and Salisa didn't remind her. But Salisa suspected that the topic of God and His will would resurface at some point during the year and, when it did, she would have to come up with better answers than the ones she had given Sophie.

# six

"Ay, mates, what do we have here?"

Sophie had forgotten their lunch date again, leaving Salisa by herself to meet all the CU staffers that came through the central office in town during the noon hour. The blue-eyed man who had just greeted her sounded Irish.

"Mike McCarter," said the man, extending his hand. "And who might ye be?"

Salisa returned his handshake. "Salisa Vrenden."

"Ah, an American," said Mike, but before he could say anything else, one of his friends stepped forward.

"And I'm Simon Llewelyn," the biggest one said. This time, Salisa thought she heard a Welsh accent.

Before another one could jump in, Salisa said, "Now, am I mistaken, or are you two from Ireland and Wales . . . respectively?" Salisa had watched Sophie comment on accents when meeting people for the first time and she didn't want to appear like a tongue-tied, culture-shocked American.

"Not bad, not bad," said another accent from behind the first two men she had met.

"And an Englishman," she announced.

"But not from England," the same voice continued. A thin but handsome sandy-haired man stepped around toward the front. "I live in Northern Ireland. Does that confuse you?"

"Yes," said Salisa, taking a chair, turning it around, and sitting on it backwards so she could still participate in the doorway conversation. "Please, explain."

"Nigel's dad is a captain in the British navy," began Simon. "So he's a born and bred Englishman. But his family's temporarily in Northern Ireland. Isn't that right, Nigel?"

"Spot on." Nigel stepped forward and bowed for Salisa.

"We're always trying to rid him of these regal behaviors," said Simon. "And that's Alan Payne," Simon pointed to the smallest man in their group. "Alan's shy, but we don't hold that against him." Salisa watched Alan as he pushed his heavy glasses back up on his nose and blushed a little.

"In fact," said Mike, "we like having Alan around because he counteracts Simon here, who says enough for the three of us." This got the men laughing again.

"You aren't by any chance a Scotsman?" asked Salisa, peeking around the three taller and bigger men to give Alan her best smile. "Because if you are, then the four of you have Great Britain nicely represented."

"Ah, we don't allow any Scots with us," Simon joked. "Alan's a Englishman like me. But he does live in England . . .Whitby, right?"

"That's right," Alan nodded, but his accent was not as polished as Nigel's.

"In any case," said Salisa, "you must all be Christians since you're wandering around in the CU office. What colleges are you from?" she asked.

"Two from Durbyfield and I'm from St. John's," said Simon, who had pointed at Mike and Alan when he said "Durbyfield."

"And I'm from Chadwick," said Nigel who had taken a seat at the far end of the office's large rectangular table. He had already started digging through the bag of books and papers he had brought with him.

"Hey, don't you have an American at Chadwick?" asked Simon. "I thought I met one. . .Bertrand or Brent or something like that."

"Bennett," said Nigel. "And he's huge! You should see how much that bloke eats for dinner!"

"He's taller than you?" asked Simon.

"He's taller than me and bigger than you," said Nigel, laying out his papers in front of him. The other three followed suit and began taking papers out of the rows of pigeonholes on the far wall. Simon returned to sit next to Salisa.

"So, where you from, Sal. . .was it Sally?"

"Salisa. I'm from Michigan, and I'm St. Anne's postgrad CU rep this year." She hoped she had used all the right lingo to describe her job.

"That's great," said Nigel from the other end of the room, not taking his eyes off the pattern he was tracing from a book. "So you came all the way from America to work with students here?"

*It's not as noble as it sounds*, Salisa thought. But she vocalized, "It's been great so far. I'm working pretty closely with Sophie Barnes. Some of you might know her from last year." Mike and Alan nodded.

"And all of you are postgrad reps, too?" Salisa inquired.

They were, and everyone continued to chat as they stapled Bible studies, filled out expense reports, or whatever else their particular CU jobs entailed. Salisa was surprised at how comfortable she was with them, and even more surprised when Mike stood up and announced that it was time for his rugby game. But rugby games were held late in the afternoon!

Salisa jumped up. She had wanted to finish reading over some students' essays before Sophie's Shakespeare rehearsal.

"I've got to run," she said, throwing her notebook and pens into her bookbag.

"You know about the meeting Saturday night, don't you?" Nigel called out after her.

"I heard something about it," Salisa said, grabbing her coat. "Isn't it that Abingdon Inter-Collegiate Christian Union meeting where all the Christian students get together in town at one of the churches?"

Simon laughed. "That's the one. But we just call it AQ, short for A-I-C-C-U. That's how we pronounce the acronym."

*That wasn't in the brochures*, Salisa thought as she headed toward the door. But Nigel beat her to it and the soft look in his hazel eyes made her pause.

"I hope I'll see you at the meeting. . . .AQ," he said. "I'd like to hear more about America. I've been there a few times with my father and it'd be fun to hear what life is like over there."

"I'm sure my stories aren't very exciting," said Salisa, trying to leave and at the same time trying to tell Nigel not to expect a lot of her history.

"I'll be the judge of that," he countered. He obviously didn't want her to go just yet. "Any American who comes across the Atlantic to serve students for a year can't be *that* boring."

Salisa blushed. Nigel's compliments were easy to take. She shifted her bookbag to her other shoulder.

"I'm really trying my best at adapting to England's culture," Salisa explained. "So I'm trying not to talk too much about home while I'm here." From their conversation that afternoon, Salisa had picked up that Nigel was some kind of a leader among his CU friends. His opinions seemed to carry great weight. She wasn't too eager to let him form an over-inflated image of her in his mind—something she'd only have to pop later if the truth about her stagnant relationship at home ever surfaced.

"It's not just America I'm interested in," persisted Nigel. Salisa was touched by his sincerity. "I'd love to hear more about your call into mission work, too," he said.

Salisa couldn't disagree with Nigel without incriminating herself. The best she could do was a warm "We'll see," as she excused herself to go take care of her other responsibilities.

"So you met the affable Mike and Alan," commented Sophie that night at tea-and-toastie time. "Alan's not very lively, but he's friendly. And I've seen them with two new ones this year. . .what'd you say their names were?"

"The Welsh one is Simon, and there's an English one who lives in Ireland. His dad's a captain in the British navy. His name is Nigel." Salisa had more questions to ask, but Sophie was sprawled out on the floor and concentrating very hard on altering one of her costumes.

"Simon's kind of big for a British guy," Salisa noted.

"Um-hm."

"And the other one you don't know. . .he's kind of tall, but thinner. I'd have to say that he's one of the best looking men I've seen around here so far."

"That's good," said Sophie, hardly looking up from the scraps of fabric she was trying to sew together. But then her head popped up and she looked up at Salisa with warm suspicion. "Since when did you take an interest in British men?"

"I'm only interested in them because they're CU colleagues," Salisa corrected.

Sophie resumed her sewing in earnest, but Salisa could tell her mind was conjuring up something. Nevertheless, she continued to fill Sophie in on bits of the afternoon's conversations. When Salisa finished talking, Sophie waited a few minutes before responding.

"Welcome to the wonderful world of CU men," she finally said.

Salisa wanted her to continue and was surprised at her own impatience. Sophie hummed a few bars of a song and then took her time biting a thread with her teeth. She seemed to realize that she had captured Salisa's interest.

"Some of the Christian men around here are as good as men can get, Salisa, and it seems like you've seen just enough of them to know what I mean. They're warm, sensitive, and funny, and some, like this Nigel you're talking about, seem to be born leaders. They're confident yet not overbearing." Sophie sighed. "It's too bad about the regulation. But then again, I guess it does prevent sticky situations. And it allows people like you and me to develop some unbelievable friendships."

"What regulation?"

Sophie looked up. "You mean you don't know?"

"No!" said Salisa.

Sophie put down her sewing. "Oh, I can't believe no one told you about it. I guess it would have been Maureen's job, but then again, maybe I was supposed to mention it. But Judith didn't say anythin' about it. . .she probably takes the whole idea for granted."

"Sophie!" Salisa almost shouted.

"It's simply an understanding," began Sophie, putting up her hand. "It's not formally written down anywhere."

"Sophie!" Salisa was yelling now. "Tell me about the regulation!"

"CU reps aren't supposed to date each other," said Sophie matter-of-factly. "They can date, just not each other." She turned her hands up and shrugged.

"That's all?"

"When you think of how much time the CU reps spend with each other you can understand why some kind of regulation is a good idea." Sophie must have thought some kind of defense was necessary. "Otherwise it's too easy to get too deep too fast."

Salisa sat back against Sophie's bed. To her, this regulation sounded strange yet sensible. But she wished somebody would have at least mentioned it to her before now, not because it would change anything about her intentions or behavior this year, but because it would have helped her understand the friendliness of people like Nigel. And Dale would have been thrilled to hear about it. He thought her lack of phone calls meant that she was forgetting all about him. And he had implied in his last letter that maybe she had gone over to England to find someone new.

"Doesn't it bother you?" asked Sophie. "I mean, if I had just learned—"

"I didn't come over here with the intention of finding a man, Sophie Barnes. So hearing about this regulation doesn't change anything. I thought you knew me better than that."

"I don't know anythin' about your intentions in that area," Sophie reminded her. "All you've told me is that you want to make a decision about this Dale back home."

Salisa started to reply but then realized that defending herself would only give Sophie more ammunition to work with.

"But I do happen to have a few intentions of my own," said Sophie slyly. "I'm in full agreement with the regulation, but I'm not keen on the idea of living like an old maid. Abingdon's Christian men are exceptional, and I plan to enjoy their company this year. What about you, Salisa? Are you with me?"

"Men are a natural part of life," replied Salisa evenly. "I don't plan to make any extra effort either to avoid or get to know them." This was evidently good news to Sophie, who was learning to use Salisa's black-and-white statements to her own advantage.

"So you'll be flexible?" she asked.

"I won't get worked up one way or the other."

Sophie resumed her humming, which again made Salisa wonder what she was contemplating.

As Salisa helped Sophie clean up her rehearsal mess that night, a funny thought struck her. What about Bennett and Hazel? The college that appointed them must not have known they were dating. Oh well, that wasn't Salisa's worry. As far as she was concerned, she was glad they had each other. At least they would leave her alone. The last people Salisa wanted to spend time with in England were clingy Americans.

# seven

"I'll have two cheese scones and some black currant juice." Salisa was ordering her favorite British lunch at Goetz's bakery one day when a familiar voice behind her interrupted.

"Oh, just give her a hamburger and some American fries ,and she'll be happy."

Salisa swung around to see Bennett, leaning up against the open doorway of the bakery and grinning.

"Bennett!" Salisa hoped her voice conveyed more excitement than she felt. "I can't believe we haven't run into each other yet," *although it's just as well,* her mind finished.

Bennett sauntered up behind her. "Well, I learned pretty quickly that our colleges are about as far apart as two colleges can get."

"You tried to come over?" asked Salisa, still not looking at him while she paid for her meal.

"Once or twice," Bennett admitted. "But for the most part I've been spending my time getting to know the people at Chadwick. And Hazel was really unhappy at first. So I spent a lot of time with her."

Salisa stayed at the counter while she put her change away, knowing that Bennett would interpret her movement toward one of the shop's small tables as an invitation to sit down.

"Hazel didn't like the hard water and the cold rooms at night and all that," said Bennett, not needing a response from Salisa to continue his story.

Involuntarily, Salisa found herself smiling. Too bad Hazel hadn't been placed at St.Anne's. Then she really would have had something to complain about!

"I was pretty miserable when I first got here, too," Salisa

found herself admitting.

"You were?"

The reminiscing began before Salisa could will it away. "My homesickness didn't last very long, though. At first my room seemed like a dungeon—actually it still does—but they've told me it will be remodeled over Christmas. That's not so long to wait. In fact, I'm kind of used to it by now." Bennett was watching her intently, so Salisa continued. "I'll miss seeing my favorite cracks on the ceiling once they repaint it. Kind of gets the imagination going as one's falling asleep. Sounds corny, but it's true."

Bennett couldn't tell whether Salisa was serious or not. "So you really like it here?" he asked.

"Love it."

"How long did it take you to figure that out?"

"About a day. And you?"

"Less than that." Bennett had that impish grin again. "I just wish Hazel could see it that way."

Bennett seemed to want to talk about Hazel, but Salisa wanted to postpone the topic for as long as she could. Sophisticated city people sometimes made Salisa feel uncomfortable, like she couldn't be herself. Somehow, Bennett didn't affect her that way. *He has a special kind of annoyance all his own*, thought Salisa. And in a weird sort of way, his enduring friendliness was starting to rub off on her.

"Bennett, I have to head over to the CU office. Are you walking that way? I'm meeting a friend over there."

"I was just going there myself when I saw you walk in here," Bennett explained with bright eyes.

*Right*, Salisa's cynical side responded. But she returned his silly grin and led the way out the door.

The CU office was just around the corner from Goetz's and as they entered, a quick glance told Salisa that Sophie had already come and gone. Salisa walked up to the center table and read Sophie's note saying she couldn't stay because she got a deal on tickets for *Twelfth Night* by the Royal Shakespeare Company. She had signed it with her now-familiar *SB* scrawl.

"That Sophie!" Salisa said aloud. Sophie never invited her along on these outings but Salisa didn't mind. Sophie seemed to sense that Salisa didn't want to spend the last sunny afternoons of autumn in a dark theater.

"Who's Sophie?" Bennett asked.

"She's the director of the Shakespeare Society this year. She was also the postgrad rep for St. Anne's last year, so she's handy to have around. She gives me lots of ideas." Salisa took a second to glance at Bennett. He was listening intently, so she went on. "She helps me with the CU job, and I help her with hers. I'm her informal assistant this year."

"You don't say." Bennett sat down at the table; he was noticeably impressed.

"And I tutor a few students in the mornings," Salisa added, succumbing to Bennett's flattering interest.

"Tutoring?"

"The professors around here like the way American students structure their essays," Salisa answered, "so I get to help them piece together all their wonderful ideas about British literature! Unfortunately, a lot of the students I see sign up for help because their professors *strongly suggest* they do so. They're not exactly the most enthusiastic group. But they're fun."

"That's great, Salisa," said Bennett. He slapped his hand lightly on the table for emphasis.

Salisa couldn't think of anything else to say, so she went over to the rows of pigeonholes on the wall and looked for notes and assignments in the "St. Anne's" box. Bennett jumped up and checked the "Chadwick" box as if suddenly remembering that this was his reason for visiting the CU office.

"I've been getting pretty involved around here myself,"

said Bennett, sitting down at the table a few chairs away from Salisa. "But it was kind of hard at first because Hazel really didn't feel comfortable here."

Hazel again! Once more Salisa squelched the prompting to let Bennett talk about what seemed to be bothering him. "So, what kind of things are you getting involved in?" she asked, hoping to steer the conversation in a different direction.

"I've been playing on some of the indoor sports teams at the Maiden Keep Sports Center," replied Bennett.

"Where's that?"

"About a mile and a half from Chadwick. . .across some of the hills at the northwest corner of Abingdon."

"Isn't that far away?"

"It's the perfect jog," Bennett replied. "I'm even getting some of the guys at Chadwick to jog with me when I go over to lift weights."

Almost instinctively, Salisa glanced over at Bennett. He had a thick sweatshirt on but it was easy to see how well built he was. Vaguely, she remembered noticing Bennett's size—and proportions—when they had first met at the airport. But now, after getting used to seeing the generally more petite English men, Bennett looked especially large.

"Good for you," said Salisa, shuffling the papers in front of her. "Exercise is a great habit." She was racking her brain to think of another non-involved question when Bennett asked a doozy.

"Hey, have you heard from home recently?" His clear green eyes and rosy, unblemished cheeks, coupled with the pointedness of his question, caused Salisa to almost stare. Bennett ran his fingers through his thick mop of hair, making the dishwater-blond waves stand almost on end. He waited.

"No, I haven't. Have you?" Salisa tried to busy herself with a questionnaire she had found in her box.

"I got a letter from your friends Ted and Ali not too long ago," Bennett said, hoping to sustain Salisa's interest.

"You did?" Salisa's tone betrayed a "Why you?" kind of answer.

Bennett didn't seem to take offense. "Ted and I got to know each other pretty well before I left," said Bennett. "He thought a year's worth of mission work was a fantastic idea, and he's been writing me once in a while to encourage me and to tell me he's praying for me."

Salisa kept her eyes and pencil on the paper in front of her. "It's hardly rough mission work, though, wouldn't you say?"

"It all depends on what you put into it," said Bennett.

Though she knew Bennett hadn't intended to hurt her feelings, Salisa felt criticized.

"And Ted said to tell you. . .if I saw you. . .that Ali wants a letter. She's written you three or four times or something like that," said Bennett. "Or if you don't have time to write, which Ali said might be the case, then you could pass on any news to me and I'll send it off in my next letter." Bennett shrugged his shoulders. "You two must have a good relationship," he said, shaking his head with mild wonder. "Hazel would hunt me down if I ever stayed away for longer than a few days without writing her."

Salisa sighed. She was tired of circumventing the subject. "So how is Hazel, Bennett? I didn't have much of a chance to talk with her when we traveled." She put her papers aside and turned toward Bennett. For the first time, Salisa saw sadness in Bennett's usually gleeful face.

"Thanks for asking, Salisa," Bennett said, looking down. "She's doing better now." He paused. "She flew home yesterday."

"Oh, Bennett, I'm sorry," Salisa said, instinctively putting her hand on Bennett's shoulder. She could feel his muscles tense with restrained emotion. She gave his shoulder a quick squeeze and then removed her hand.

Bennett's smile returned. "Thanks for caring, Salisa. But I'll be okay. It's probably better this way. Everything about this place made her unhappy and as much as I tried to empathize with her, I couldn't find anything I disliked. I just wish it didn't have to be this way."

Salisa nodded sympathetically. She really did feel sorry for Bennett, but she couldn't say that she was devastated because of Hazel's departure.

"Besides," Bennett laughed. "We just found out that CU reps aren't supposed to date each other!" His smile and shaking head masked his grief. "So you see, there's a lot that might work out for the better. And Hazel even had a job waiting for her."

"What kind of job?"

"I guess Hazel had been asking her parents to keep an eye out for teaching jobs just in case she returned, and one turned up in a place called Pepperton." When he said the town's name aloud, a look of recognition swept across Bennett's face.

"Hey! Isn't that where you're from. . .and where Ted and Ali bought their house?"

Salisa couldn't believe it. She knew the teacher Hazel would be replacing; she was having her first child and was prone to all sorts of sicknesses. She must have given in to bedrest just when Hazel's availability became known.

"It's a small world," Salisa said with a deadpan face. As glad as she was to be away from Pepperton, having someone like Hazel there while she was gone disturbed her.

"Hey, Salisa, are you okay?" Bennett's kind eyes were leaning in toward hers.

"Don't be silly, Bennett. I should be asking you that. You look like you're doing great, but it must be tough. You and Hazel were kind of serious, weren't you?" Salisa hadn't intended to get so personal with Bennett, but it had just come out.

"We weren't as close as Hazel would have liked," said Bennett. His shoulders, square as they were, slumped a little. "But it seemed like we had a lot in common."

Salisa had a few more questions in mind but resisted asking them. She and Bennett had gotten chummy enough. She didn't want to imply that they should become good friends simply because they knew some of the same people back home. Bennett was an outgoing, attractive man; he wouldn't have any problem finding friends to fill the time he had previously spent trying to placate Hazel.

"Well, I'm sure your year will turn out all right," Salisa reassured him. "And I'm glad you filled me in about Hazel. But I have a few more things to do this afternoon. . . ." Salisa gathered the papers she had collected from her box. "It was great running into you, Bennett. Take care."

"I'll see you Saturday night, right?" Bennett asked as she neared the door. "It's the first AQ meeting of the year, isn't it?"

"I think so," Salisa replied. "Everyone keeps asking me about it." With her hand on the doorknob, she glanced back at Bennett. "I'll look for you there. Goodbye."

On her way to the English building, Salisa regretted making promises she didn't want to keep. Oh, well. Maybe she would run into Mike, Alan, Simon, and Nigel before—or instead of—Bennett. That thought made her smile.

People were already milling about the white stone church when Salisa and Sophie entered Abingdon's old Market Square that Saturday night. St. Oswald's had its own private corner sandwiched between the Square's tallest brick stores, and students were stamping the slush off their feet and brushing the light snowfall out of their hair before they entered. When Salisa and Sophie followed them in, the smell of cold stone and dusty corners mixed with the scent of wet coats and hair.

"The dampness around here sinks into everything, doesn't it, Sophie?" But Sophie had already found some old friends and was motioning for Salisa to follow. Salisa tagged along, saying "Hi yas" to those she knew and a few she didn't. The pews and lines of folding chairs in St. Oswald's filled up quickly, and Salisa watched as Nigel walked up to the foot-high platform in the center of the building.

"Welcome back, second- and third-year reps," Nigel's exquisite yet deep voice bellowed through the second-rate microphones. St. Oswald's stone-and-plaster walls obviously had not been built with electronic acoustics in mind. "And a very special welcome to first-year reps and anyone else who is with us here tonight for the first time. If you'd all just find a seat, we will get started. There'll be plenty of time to mill about afterward, and it'd be great if we all started venturing out to each other's colleges more during the week anyway." Nigel caught Salisa's eye and quickly added, "And welcome to the Americans we have scattered among us. . .I know there are a few of them here." Salisa saw a hand pop up from a group near Nigel. It was Bennett's, and Salisa watched Nigel return the American "high five" sign.

"For those Americans who are undergrads," Nigel continued, "we'll welcome you as juniors and seniors, which is probably what you are. If you haven't figured out that we Brits get our degree in three years instead of four, see me afterward and I'll explain it all to you." A ripple of chuckling went through the crowd, and Nigel had a few more lighthearted things to say about the differences between Americans and "Brits," as they called themselves. Salisa wasn't sure what he was getting at until she saw him pull Bennett up by the hand to the platform.

"I'd like to ask one of the Americans—a new friend, I might add—to open with a prayer tonight," said Nigel. He gave Bennett an affectionate hug with his free arm.

"It never ceases to amaze me," Nigel said, as the group

grew quiet, "that the bond among Christians can be so strong." A few soft "Amens" went up from the crowd. "Here's a person who is very different from me," said Nigel, holding his hand out toward Bennett. "When I first met him, he had never had a proper four o'clock tea, and he tried to tell me that coffee tasted better than even our best Earl Grey tea!" Laughter broke out among the responsive crowd.

"But lately we've been having some good chats," continued Nigel, "and I'm amazed to see how similar we really are. We all face the same struggles when we try to share our faith with other people, and we all feel strengthened when we find those with whom we have Christ in common."

"Despite the quirks of our different cultures," added Bennett, leaning down into the microphone.

"That's right," said Nigel. "Despite the quirks of coffee and tea and all that. So, without further commentary. . .," he handed Bennett the mike.

"Dear Lord," said Bennett, and Salisa immediately sensed the bowing of heads around her. She was surprised by the flatness of Bennett's voice compared to Nigel's.

"It's great to be here and to taste the kind of fellowship I'm sure we're all anticipating. . .heaven. Here we are, some of us Americans and most of us from Great Britain, and some from even farther around the world. But all we feel now is excitement about being together. Thanks for the time we're going to have worshiping You and getting to know a little bit more about Your Word. Bless this year at the CU here in Abingdon." Salisa watched him squint his eyes and purse his lips with feeling. "And help us never to take each other and the salvation You've given us for granted. Help us to be salt and light throughout Abingdon and wherever You may take us." Salisa heard more soft "Amens."

"In Jesus' name," finished Bennett, "Amen." Again, more "Amens."

Salisa wasn't used to expressing her faith audibly in a

large group but as the evening progressed, she felt herself opening up more and more. She clapped enthusiastically when the group sang, and she nodded and mouthed "Amen" along with those around her whenever the different speakers said something she especially liked. And she didn't want to get up from her knees after the last prayer—another new experience for Salisa.

"So, what'd you think?" Nigel asked, walking up to her almost immediately after the meeting ended. Soft guitar music from the front mingled with clusters of conversations.

"I thought it was great!"

"Well, then you'll probably like the postgrad meeting even better," said Nigel, his eyes darting around for other postgrads to remind. "Can you make your way over to the side room over there as soon as you can? We'll make it quick."

Salisa found the room Nigel had pointed out, catching up with Sophie on the way. Nigel hadn't been boasting—the smaller group meeting was full of moving prayer and instant rapport with the other CU leaders. Nigel was warm but almost businesslike in his announcements, and the group appreciated the booklet of administrative procedures that he had put together for them. It was too late in the evening to listen to a long list of details.

"So have a good look at this during the next month," Nigel finished quickly. "We'll meet again after the next AQ meeting."

The group dispersed and began breaking into small groups of people that Salisa knew would be going off for tea and more deep conversation. She turned to look for her coat, and she saw Bennett walking toward her.

"Can I interest you in joining me for some tea?" he asked. He seemed to be almost glowing from all the praying he had been doing that evening. "I'm not the coffeeholic Nigel made me out to be!"

When Salisa didn't respond right away, Bennett said, "That's okay, Salisa. You don't have to. All I really wanted to do was to thank you for the other day. I really needed some company. . .some American company it seemed. . .and I appreciated your sitting there and just listening for a while."

"No problem, Bennett. I didn't really do anything." Salisa was starting to feel mildly embarrassed about her earlier intolerance of him. "Well, that's all I wanted to say," he said, giving her one of those rich, dimpled grins that had so caught her attention when she had first traveled with him.

"No problem," Salisa repeated, but this time something about Bennett made her stare a little longer. She quickly reprimanded herself for getting so caught up in Bennett's good looks. She had never been the type to gawk before and she certainly wasn't going to start now.

She deliberately began looking around for Sophie and quickly located her in a corner, talking to Nigel. Nigel must have sensed someone staring at him because he turned toward Salisa and Bennett and waved. Salisa watched as Nigel tipped his head as he pointed toward Salisa and Bennett. Sophie responded by grabbing her coat and following him across the room.

"What do you say we all have tea together at my place?" asked Nigel cheerily. "Sophie here was just telling me that she had an American friend, and I thought the two of you might like to meet. But I see you already have."

"Actually, we traveled over here together," offered Bennett.

"Oh, really?" asked Sophie, turning to Salisa with wide eyes. "You didn't tell me that."

Nigel seemed relieved to know that he wasn't the only one who thought Salisa was secretive. "I'm sure there's a lot that we don't know about each other yet," said Nigel pleasantly. "And I can't think of a threesome that I'd rather spend time with and get to know better." Nigel lightly placed his hands on Salisa's and Bennett's shoulders. "Can I convince you two Americans. . .and Sophie. . .to come over for a spot of tea?"

Sophie answered for Salisa by pulling her along and Bennett didn't need to be asked twice. Both he and Nigel looked quite pleased with the arrangement.

# eight

"I haven't enjoyed the company of two men more in ages," whispered Sophie as soon as they left Chadwick's main dormitory that Saturday night. She turned to give a pair of men in a third-floor window one last wave. "But you," she said, turning back around and poking her gloved finger into Salisa's arm, "were a proper stick in the mud! Two charmin' men invite us to tea, and you mope about as if they'd sent you to the tower! Whatever is wrong with you?"

Salisa tried to think of something that would appease Sophie. "I'm just tired, that's all, Soph."

"Nice try. Guess again."

Salisa gave Sophie her best blank look.

"Don't try ignorance on me either," Sophie said as she put her arm in Salisa's. "You're always good until at least midnight. Your ten-thirty yawn was a fake. . .and a poor one at that." She gave her silent friend a playful hug.

"I'm afraid you're going to have to be more honest with me as time goes on," said Sophie. "What's botherin' you? I can't read your mind, you know."

Salisa took a deep breath. It was too late to deflect Sophie's interest now. She was on the hunt. And Salisa had watched Sophie pursue a truth, an answer, or even a stage interpretation until she found it.

"It's just that I didn't come here to spend time with Americans," Salisa finally revealed. "And Bennett is an American."

A light bulb went on in Sophie's head. "So that's it! I could tell he bothered you, but I didn't know why. I just figured it had somethin' to do with you and what's-her-name?

58

The one Nigel kept mentioning."

"Hazel. But it has nothing to do with Hazel." Salisa had more important things to worry about. "It's just Americans in general."

"Well, that's a silly way to look at things." But now that Salisa had answered her question, Sophie resumed her analysis of what she kept calling a "brilliant evening."

Salisa let her chatter a while, but Sophie's increasing excitement worried her. She didn't want Sophie to think that late-night tea with Bennett and Nigel needed to become a regular event.

"Soph," she interrupted, "let's not make such a big deal about this. We had fun with Bennett and Nigel. Maybe we'll run into them at the CU office during the week. Bennett tells good jokes and Nigel brings spiritual stories and a nice cultural background into the picture. Why can't we just leave it at that?"

"Because relationships like these never just stay at that, Salisa." Sophie's black eyes were fiery. "Sooner or later people get involved. And because it can't be romantic, people start developing all sorts of exciting ways to be together. Don't question me on this, Salisa. I've seen it happen. And I think all the necessary ingredients are there with Bennett and Nigel."

Salisa was glad that Sophie couldn't see her roll her eyes. She respected Sophie's enthusiasm for Shakespeare, but she couldn't understand why she got so giddy whenever they were around men. The more handsome the men were, the more silly Sophie became.

"You're completely overreacting, Sophie," said Salisa. "It's late, and I think you've put a little too much caffeine into your system. You'll be back to your old rational self in the morning." Salisa paused and then added. "Even if I were interested in spending more time with Nigel and Bennett, I still couldn't do it. I can't get involved with anyone else until I figure out what I'm supposed to do about Dale."

"Who said anything about getting involved with some-one?" asked Sophie. "There are many gradations in the game of relationships, Salisa. It's not always as either/or as you make it. And," Sophie hesitated, as if weighing her words carefully, "I wouldn't be surprised if this situation at home is more your fault than Dale's and that you really aren't as stuck as you make it out to be."

Salisa stared at her friend. As much as she disliked Sophie's bluntness, sometimes it hit on enough truth that she couldn't be mad at her. But she tried her best to sound offended. "How can you make accusations like that, Sophie? All you know about Dale and the others back home is what I tell you, and I don't tell you much."

"Talking to more people about your life back home might help you keep it in an accurate focus," replied Sophie.

*You're the one who lets things get out of focus!* Salisa wanted to say. But she held her tongue.

They didn't talk much as they turned down the final gravel path toward St. Anne's. They stuck with small talk—tomorrow's rehearsal and the next St. Anne's Bible study night. But when Salisa took out her key and held the door open for Sophie, she asked meekly, "You really don't think I'm being honest with myself?" Slowly, she was starting to think that maybe Sophie *could* see something that she couldn't.

"As honest as you can be," said Sophie, "at this point." She smiled. "Now, get off to bed before we get into one of our famous pillow fights or somethin'."

Quicker than Salisa could prepare for it, Sophie took off her wet gloves and bonked Salisa on the head with them. With a giggle, she ran up the dark staircase ahead of Salisa and down the corridor that led to her room.

"It's salt in your cereal tomorrow when you aren't look-ing, Sophie Barnes," Salisa called out after her. "Be on your guard!" Her voice bounced off the brick walls around her and Salisa hoped Miss Pendrill wouldn't come storming out one of the hall's offices to yell at her.

But the building was silent. As she climbed the stairs slowly and quietly, Salisa thought she heard Sophie chuckling just before she heard a door slam. Sophie was turning into a good, if tactless, friend. If spending time with Bennett was a way to spend more time with Sophie—and Nigel— then Salisa was just going to have to go along with it.

"How'd your session go?" Salisa asked a week later when Sophie came bounding into the CU office. "I heard from some of my tutorial students that your presentation on *A Midsummer Night's Dream* was the best lecture they've had all year!" Salisa was trying hard to stay on good terms with Sophie. She didn't want Sophie to tire of her strange reservations about home and Bennett.

"The students were brilliant," gushed Sophie. "Almost all of them had acted in school Shakespeare classes, and their questions were penetrating. They all had an excellent grasp of Shakespearean themes and even gave me some ideas for stage interpretations."

"I'm really proud of you, Soph," said Salisa, standing to reach over and give Sophie a friendly hug. Sophie returned it, but then quickly resumed one of her characteristic lilts around the room. Salisa was starting to learn that Sophie acted like this whenever she was in a really good mood.

"So, do you need some help this afternoon?" Salisa asked. "How are the props coming along? I could paint or something."

"I think the painting's all under control—for at least a while," Sophie answered, almost too nonchalantly. "But there is something else I'd like you to do." She had come to a stop near the far wall and was browsing through the St. Anne's pigeonhole.

"What?" Sophie's tone and mood were making Salisa suspicious.

"But it's not job related."

"What are you getting at, Barnes?"

"Well, Bennett came to the seminar today, and—"

"Bennett? Since when has he had an interest in Shakespeare?"

"He said he was in town for a meeting, and when he saw the notices about the seminar, he thought it was somethin' we'd both be at. So he just came to say hi."

"If he just came to say hi, you wouldn't be acting so weird," objected Salisa. "What is it you want to ask me?"

Sophie couldn't stop from smiling any longer. "It's no big deal, Salisa. It's just that I promised Bennett that we'd make Nigel and him dinner tomorrow night."

"You what?"

"You don't have to be there if you don't want," Sophie said, then turned around to mutter, "although I certainly don't know why you wouldn't want to be."

"It's just that I'm starting to feel like I don't get to make any decisions around here," said Salisa, catching the whine in her throat before it had a chance to escape. "That's why I came over here. . .to practice making some decisions on my own."

This made Sophie angry. "I don't know what it is you're carryin' around with you that's makin' you so difficult to get along with, but I for one am glad of the friendships we're makin'. So, if you don't want to be a part of them, just say so!"

Salisa slumped in one of the CU office's more comfortable chairs. Sophie was right; she was being ridiculous. But she still felt somewhat justified in her frustration. She hadn't wanted to spend much time with Bennett and here they were cooking dinner for him! Didn't only good friends do that for each other? But deep down, Salisa knew she should be thankful for Sophie's social skills—and her patience in keeping Salisa included.

"Okay, Barnes," she conceded. "Count me in. Will you forgive an American's silly stubbornness?"

Sophie came over to sit on the arm of the chair in which Salisa was sitting. A mischievous grin came over her face as she put her arm around Salisa's shoulders.

"If you give me a chance to explain what I need you to do this afternoon."

Salisa grudgingly returned the squeeze. "How can I say no to a twirp like you?"

"What's a twirp?" asked Sophie, not sure whether she should be offended or not.

"In this case, it's a term of endearment," said Salisa.

"Splendid!" Sophie jumped up. "I need you to go to Mark and Spencer's this afternoon to pick up a few things for the dinner. I have to rehearse with the lead characters today and tomorrow, so I won't have time to shop." She seemed to have switched into high gear as soon as she finished the task of convincing Salisa that dinner was a good idea.

"You knew you would be able to persuade me about dinner, didn't you?" Salisa couldn't help but like Sophie's cocky confidence.

"Actually," said Sophie between mouthfuls of her dry sandwich, "I was only sure of one thing: that you'd object. So, at least I was prepared."

"You are getting to know me pretty well, Barnes." Salisa paused. "And you don't mind my dragging my feet when it comes to some of your fly-by-night plans?"

"I like you more than ever," said Sophie, smiling. "Do you think I'm always one to agree with everythin' that crosses my path? Not at all!"

"A woman after my own heart," said Salisa. "Although two stubborn women in the same room could be dangerous. So, if you'll excuse me, I have some shopping to do." Sophie ripped out a handwritten grocery list from her notebook and waved Salisa off with a smile.

"It'll be fun. You'll see!"

If Sophie were there, Salisa knew it would be.

"Who would have thought that a concoction called 'toad-in-the-holes' could be so tasty!" Bennett was impressed with Sophie's cooking skills, as they all were. Dinner was going smoothly and Salisa couldn't believe she was having such a good time. What was even more amazing was that Salisa was starting not to mind Bennett. Rather than being the American she feared would tag along and ruin her year abroad by constant reminders of life "back home," Bennett was actually bringing more British culture into her life—Nigel.

As the foursome talked and teased each other in St. Anne's guest kitchen that night, Nigel entertained his friends with stories from India, Canada, Africa—all countries of the former British Commonwealth. His father had kept the family together wherever he was stationed, and Nigel was now the richer for it. Sophie and Salisa sat engrossed, wishing they could relate to some of the scenes Nigel was describing.

"Well, I intend to do some traveling during the five weeks' worth of Christmas holidays coming up," said Salisa. "I'm sure it won't be as exotic as what Nigel has been talking about, but it will be fun."

"You're not going home for Christmas?" asked Bennett.

"Oh, no," responded Salisa. "I've made plans with the university law department to go with a student group to Russia for a week. And Sophie has kindly offered to help me plan a trip through the parts of England I haven't seen yet."

"And help her fit in all the offers she's had to visit the homes of the people she's met," Sophie added.

"It's no big deal," Salisa started explaining once she had caught Bennett's questioning eyebrows. "You two probably know some of the people I'm visiting—Simon Llewelyn from Wales and Fiona Irvine from Scotland. Those are the two I'll be staying with the longest."

"Who's going to show you around Ireland?" asked Nigel. "It seems as if you have all the rest of the countries covered."

"Nobody's asked," said Salisa. "The only Irishman I know fairly well is Mike McCarter, and I think he's traveling around Europe with his family for most of the holidays."

"Well, it's settled then," said Nigel.

"What's settled?"

"You'll come visit me for a while."

A trapped feeling began to creep over Salisa. Sophie sensed it and came to her rescue.

"I'll help you figure it in. . .if you want, Salisa," she said. Then she turned to Nigel. "You understand, however, that we've been working on these plans for a while now, and it might be harder than you think to simply rearrange the trip."

"I understand," said Nigel, dipping his head with politeness. This relieved Salisa and she threw her friend a grateful glance for getting the "might be too hard to reschedule" idea into the discussion. Salisa now knew that she would *probably* accept. Though it shouldn't have been that important to her, having some say in the matter helped a lot.

"Just let me know a few days before the term's over," said Nigel. Then he added, "Whatever you decide is fine," without any prompting from Sophie.

Before anyone could start another topic of conversation, Sophie pushed her plate away and stood up from the table. "Who's up for a walk?" she asked. When she didn't get the immediate enthusiasm she wanted, she added, "Well, I'm not about to dish out any of my famous fruitcake unless my guests have worked up a proper appetite for it first. We'll come back for tea—and coffee for the Americans if they want."

"It'll be tea for me," said Salisa, getting up with the others. "Don't you know how hard I'm working at fitting into British culture?"

"That's just it," Bennett said lightheartedly. "You work too hard at it. I hadn't ever intended to like tea the way they drink it over here—almost white with milk. But now I like it. I guess it all kind of rubs off on you when you spend time with polished British people like Nigel."

"Well, I appreciate Salisa's effort," said Sophie as she put the dishes in the sink and began rinsing them off. She was pleased to see both Bennett and Nigel helping Salisa clear the table.

"See what nice men these two are," whispered Sophie as she and Salisa went to the corner of the room to retrieve the coats and scarves from the coat rack.

"I don't give them enough credit, do I?"

"Nope. But you're learning."

"Thanks to you," whispered Salisa. She gave Sophie a quick kiss on the cheek before they returned to the men waiting for them in the doorway.

# nine

"Nigel, this is charming!" Salisa plopped down on the bed of the guest room to which Nigel had just led her. The swirling in her stomach was finally subsiding, and Salisa was beginning to think the long train and ferry rides to Ireland had been worth it.

"So you like it?" he asked. Nigel had been the perfect travel companion. He didn't have the same need for conversation that someone like Bennett did, and Salisa had been able to weather her seasickness in silence. Although she could have done with a little more sympathy from him, his hospitality was quickly causing her to forget her earlier traveling miseries.

"I don't just like it, Nigel, I love it. You have to remember that this is the first room I'll have slept in since coming to England that isn't drafty and musty and turquoise." The guest room had two twin beds in it, each with plush calico comforters and an assortment of unique, embroidered throw pillows. Salisa had a space heater by her bed and an empty hot water bottle on her nightstand. The adjoining private bathroom had an oil lamp, soft, powder blue towels, and a sparkling, old-fashioned bathtub. Salisa tried to inhale the comfort all around her. Nigel's mother must have lit several potpourri candles just before she arrived, and the room smelled like cinnamon and gingerbread all mixed together.

"Can I. . .just enjoy this for a while?" Salisa asked. Her room at St. Anne's didn't bother her any more, but suddenly Salisa was reminded of how good it felt to curl up in a clean room where warmth, softness, and pleasant aromas were readily available. There was even a basket of fresh fruit on the dresser, waiting to be sampled.

Nigel was enjoying Salisa's reaction to the room. "You go right ahead," he said, fluffing one of her pillows for her. "Dinner will be at seven o'clock in the sitting room, but feel free to wander around before then if you're ready."

"Thanks, Nigel." She felt like jumping up and throwing her arms around him but knew that this outburst of emotion would probably make him uncomfortable. As he walked toward the door, Salisa remembered a question she had postponed asking during the hour-long car ride into Belfast with Nigel and his father.

"Nigel?" she asked.

He quickly turned around with a look that told Salisa he was ready to go get whatever else she might need.

"I was just wondering about your relationship with your father." She was learning from Sophie how to get right to the point. "You were both so quiet in the car. Are you sure it's okay that I'm here? I don't want to upset any family routines or anything like that."

"No, not at all," he said, surprised at Salisa's question. He had to think for a while before he continued. "I can see that you haven't had much exposure to polite British family life, now have you?" asked Nigel, smiling.

Salisa shook her head.

"I suppose my dad's worse than most because of his job. He's a good captain because he's that way."

"I can imagine," murmured Salisa, although she still didn't see that degree of composure as positively as Nigel did. Nigel's father had looked like an older Nigel, as Salisa had thought he might, but his face was harder and more chiseled in certain places. Despite the comfort of her room, Salisa was starting to have reservations about living with a very precise, formal British family for five straight days.

"Well, if you're sure it's all right," Salisa said tentatively. "Do they like guests? I mean, especially foreigners like me?"

Nigel's smile was one of assurance. "They love guests, Salisa. Especially foreign ones. We're all aiming to treat you like a queen while you're here—with no offense to Elizabeth and the Queen Mum, of course."

"Thanks, Nigel. I'll do my best to be a worthy guest."

"I'm sure you will be," he replied. And then he left her to enjoy her room.

As often as she could that week, Salisa sat on the twin bed nearer to the window and let the view of the Irish country-side inspire and soothe her. Nigel's back yard was full of rocks and small ledges of flowers that fell away into green hills that were obscured by mist in some places. It was that scene that came most often to Salisa's mind during the lonely ten nights she later spent in Russia. She hadn't really known any of the law students she was traveling with, and since thirteen girls were part of the tour group, one ended up roomming alone—Salisa.

On one hand, she was enjoying the time at night to think, write letters, and read the few books she had brought along. But on the other hand, time alone to think was the last thing Salisa needed right now. Her mind was a whirl of thoughts of home, excitement for a second term at Abingdon, and a strange warmth in her stomach when she thought of her time with Nigel in Ireland.

Each Irish memory would begin with her first glimpse through the window of Nigel's guest room. After Nigel had left her alone to rest up after their trip, she had opened the draperies, stared at the scenery until she fell asleep, and awakened several hours later full of replenished vigor. She had wandered out into the cold, dark central hall of the house, which was actually more like a big empty room, and had followed the sound of voices and a crack of light to a door diagonally across from her bedroom. When she had tapped on the door, a chorus of posh voices had echoed, "Come in!" Warmth, brightness, and the strong smell of curry had bombarded Salisa's senses.

"Welcome to the sitting room," Nigel had exclaimed. "Did you have a good rest?"

Salisa had nodded and quickly glanced from Nigel to his parents and then back to Nigel's comforting smile again. Nigel's father was casually dressed but still sat like a soldier, and his mother had a formal dress and heels on and a fancy scarf in her hair. Though they had intimidated her at first, Salisa had quickly discovered that Nigel's parents were as charming and clever as Nigel had told her they would be and as politely interested in Salisa as she was in them. Conversation with the Worthingtons was going to be stimulating and delightfully proper. Within a matter of minutes, Salisa had even found herself adopting some of their expressions and airs.

Each night, Nigel had insisted on doing the dishes for his parents, and Salisa had always helped out. During these dishwashing sessions, Salisa and Nigel had tracked any loose ends from the dinner hour's conversations and planned their nightly trek into Belfast. Then they would come home in time to have a late-night cup of tea with Nigel's parents. It was a lovely routine, and Salisa found herself wishing it would last forever! Lazy days and interesting, peaceful nights. Around eleven o'clock or so, Nigel's parents would go to bed, leaving Nigel and Salisa alone in the sitting room. The embers in the fireplace would slowly die, the late hour preventing Nigel and Salisa from throwing on more wood.

Eventually it had happened. After a night or two of shivering from opposite ends of the couch as they talked, Nigel had finally voiced what they both were thinking. "Why don't you curl up here with me while we wait for the fire to go out?" In response, Salisa had dragged her blanket over to his side of the couch and had leaned up against him.

"See? I don't bite," he had said.

"I didn't think you did," responded Salisa. "But I just wonder how sensible we're being—two CUers snuggling together in a dark room!"

Nigel had only squeezed her a little harder. "I have nothing but the most noble intentions around you, Salisa Vrenden. I hope you realize that."

"You haven't given me reason to think otherwise."

"Have I given you reason to think anything?"

A practical answer came to Salisa. "Of course you have, Nigel. You're always giving inspiring talks. I learn a lot from you." She paused. "Is that what you mean?"

"Somewhat," he said. "Anything else?"

Salisa debated a moment. "Well, your commitment to be a missionary makes me think hard about my own life."

"In what way?"

Salisa again tried to phrase her words carefully. "People like you make me feel like a second-rate Christian."

"What?"

"I knew that probably wouldn't come out right." Salisa turned a little so she could look Nigel right in the eyes. "It's just that I don't know if I have the same level of commitment people like you and Sophie have. Don't get me wrong. I'm not out to be the world's greatest Christian or anything like that. I guess I just know myself well. . .and all my rotten reasons for doing things."

"Salisa," said Nigel, tilting her chin up to his face. "What are you talking about?"

In reliving the memory while sitting alone in Russia, Salisa suspected that they must have looked pretty romantic: Nigel was holding Salisa, who was all wrapped up in blankets, and tipping her face up to his. But at the time, Salisa was thinking of anything but romance. Instead, she was caught up in trying to explain her way out of Nigel's questions without giving too much of her home history away. So, the moment faded and Salisa ended up telling him the barest minimum about how she ended up in England.

Nigel patiently listened while Salisa told him about a "vague sort of restlessness" that had spurred her on to apply for the position in England. "It hasn't been what I would call a real sacrifice," she concluded.

"But Salisa," Nigel had said when she was finished, "I don't see it that way at all. Why, you're farther away from home than I would be from any of the places I'm thinking about going to as a missionary. How can you say that what you've done doesn't show some degree of character and reliance upon God's will?"

Salisa felt odd arguing about her own virtue, so she let Nigel think what he would.

"What about you, Nigel?" Salisa had finally prompted, attempting to turn the conversation around to him. "Why are you so interested in mission work?"

"It's quite simple, really," said Nigel. "Some Christians took a genuine interest in me when I was an Oxford snob and, in the process, I found God. My life became completely different—different goals, more satisfying friendships, more peace. So now I have a heart for students who are like I was five years ago. I'd like to go to some of the places I told you about. . .maybe India or Kenya. . .but I have a hard time thinking about leaving my homeland. I'm British to the core! Even living in Ireland during the holidays tests my mettle."

"So that's why you think it's no small feat to live for a year away from a home in America." Salisa had turned back around and was leaning against Nigel.

"I don't think, my dear, I *know*." With that, Nigel had kissed her lightly on the back of the head.

For a few moments, neither one of them had spoken. Then, Nigel had whispered softly in her ear, "Maybe others see strengths in you that you don't, Salisa. Sometimes I watch you interact with the students, and I'm amazed at how quickly they identify with you and warm up to you." Then

he had paused, and his voice had deepened with seriousness. "Don't underestimate the ways God is using you,
Salisa, and don't close your eyes to what God may be trying to tell you during your year at Abingdon."

Those whispered words of Nigel's haunted Salisa during
the long hours of darkness in Russia. She was cold and lonely
,and memories of her time in Ireland grew in proportion the
more she stirred them up. She even wrote Dale a letter saying that it was over, that she had found someone else, and
he would have six months to get over her by the time she
would return.

But would she return to Pepperton if that someone was
Nigel? Anxiously, Salisa ripped up her letter to Dale. Something inside her wanted to keep him waiting for her just a
little longer. Marrying a British missionary was too drastic
a remedy for even the worst case of restlessness, Salisa
quickly decided.

Or was it?

# ten

Nothing had ever tasted so good as the first cup of hot tea Salisa had upon returning to her room at St. Anne's! And never had her room looked so cozy and inviting! It was still musty and drafty, but the holiday remodelers had left her with peach walls, a new cream-colored comforter and pillow, and perhaps best of all, a shade for the light.

Salisa sat on her bed and leaned against the clean, blank wall. A strange sense of loss began to creep over her. Who would have thought that she'd miss her old decor. She had managed to make her old room homey with plenty of photos from home and the bright red curtains Sophie had sewn together for her. Now, upon a closer inspection, the room was almost *too* cheery for Salisa who liked to retreat to dreary hideaways when she was in the mood to write letters or think. And Sophie's red curtains were gone, replaced by a pale, flowery pattern that offered no noticeable contrast to the freshly painted walls.

Salisa leaned forward to pick up the pile of photos the painters had removed from her wall and left on the nightstand. These, she hoped, would help in recovering her room's original character. Then she remembered the rolls of holiday photos she had brought back with her from her travels. Salisa found the packet in her backpack, and then sat back down on her bed, intending to spread out the photos and pick her favorites from each stack.

The photos she looked for first were of her time in Ireland. The first picture she came to was of her and Nigelstanding in front of Christmas decorations in downtown Belfast. Again, she felt a strange lurch in her stomach.

What was going on between her and Nigel? *Probably nothing,* she rebuked herself. *I'm getting as bad as Sophie!* Quickly she sorted through her old photos and found one of her and Dale. No lurch. In fact, seeing Dale's sincere grin and his strong, big arm around her waist only intensified her guilt for putting him through so much. What right did she have to be so happy while he was so miserable? How could she return to Pepperton and break this man's heart?

To get her mind off the situation, Salisa found photos of her and Sophie and some of the friends she had visited during her Christmas travels and put these on her wall in place of any that had either Nigel or Dale in them.

Salisa didn't remember dozing off, but she must have. When a knock at her door made her open her eyes, the room was dark. It had also grown colder.

"Who is it?" Salisa tried to sound awake.

There was a few seconds' hesitation before a familiar voice said, "Guess who?"

Salisa knew she recognized the man's voice, but it didn't sound like Nigel. He was the only one who knew she was planning to return to Abingdon a few days early.

"Can you give me a clue?" Salisa stood up and grabbed a sweater.

"If I say any more, you'll realize that I don't have an ac—"

"Bennett!" Salisa opened the door cautiously. "What are you doing back so early?"

"I was about to ask you the same thing," he said. Bennett looked well fed and well rested, and Salisa supposed she looked just the opposite: she knew she was run down from nursing the cold she had caught in Russia. But the look on Bennett's face told her that he was glad to see her anyway. She struggled to remember whether she had left Abingdon disliking or liking Bennett. Positive memories told her the latter.

"Well, are you going to let me in?"

Salisa opened the door a little wider. "Sure, come on in," she said with an apologetic smile. As Bennett walked past her, Salisa glanced behind him into the darkened hallway. "Hmm. They haven't put on all the lights and heat yet," she murmured, mostly to herself. "And weren't the front doors locked?"

"Actually, they were," said Bennett, putting his wet coat on the back of Salisa's desk chair and taking a seat. "I walked in with a gray-haired lady. . .kind of thin—"

"Pendrill," said Salisa dryly. "Just what she needs to see— a man entering St. Anne's."

"But I think she liked me."

"What makes you think so?" Salisa was readying her tea-kettle to fix Bennett a cup of tea.

"I just smiled at her and told her I had seen a friend's light on. Then I said as sweetly as I could, 'Would it be all right if I visited her for a few minutes?' "

Salisa cocked her head and studied the sweet expression Bennett was demonstrating for her. It disarmed Salisa as well.

"Ah, Bennett," Salisa clicked her tongue. "You're too handsome for your own good. To think that you can even charm Pendrill with so much as a wink. And she's not the only one. You don't know how many St. Anne girls keep asking about you whenever you and Nigel come and visit."

"You've got to be kidding."

"No, seriously."

The water in the kettle was starting to send steam through its spout. "Do you want anything in your tea?" Salisa asked. "I have fresh milk on the windowsill, but if you want powdered skim, I have that as well."

"Hey, where'd you get that electric teakettle?" Bennett asked, incredulously. "I just realized that I'm in an American's room. You're not supposed to have one of those!"

"I would certainly hope that other Americans took it upon themselves to practice British hospitality while they live here!" Salisa responded with mock indignation. "But I have to admit that it was my Bible study group's idea. They gave it to me for Christmas right before I left. Now, do you want your tea white or black?"

Bennett shifted back on the chair. He had a sheepish look on his face and Salisa couldn't figure it out.

"What is it, Bennett?"

"It's just that I've been in America for the last four weeks. I'm drinking coffee again like most red-blooded Americans."

Salisa tried to sound stern. "But you're in England now. And when with Brits, do as the Brits do! I know I've told you that before."

"But I'm not with a Brit."

"But I try to do as the Brits do, and since you're in my room, you'll follow my rules." She reached for a small carton on her windowsill and poured a bit of milk into a steaming cup of tea.

"Tsk, tsk," said Bennett, taking the cup from Salisa. "Somebody's gotten frisky during the holidays."

"You would have, too, if you had sat through ten lonely nights in a hotel in Russia the only options being wandering around on dark streets in twenty-degree-below-zero temperatures or partying with students you hardly knew." Salisa tried to sound traumatized, but when she looked at Bennett, his pretend pout, complete with a bottom lip sticking out, made her laugh. She tried to turn away from him, but he caught sight of her stifling a laugh.

"You're so funny, Salisa," he said. "One minute you're bullying me around, and the next you're begging for my sympathy."

Salisa was amused despite her best efforts not to be. "Okay. So it wasn't all that bad. But I wasn't expecting to be with such a wild bunch. Oh, well. Chalk it up to experience." Salisa held out both cups of tea for Bennett to take, which he did without question. She positioned herself on the end of her bed and then reached for her tea. But she leaned too far and, as she did, she almost fell into Bennett, spilling her tea as she went.

"Whoa!" Bennett exclaimed, holding Salisa up with his left arm as he raised his tea in his right hand to keep it from spilling too.

Pushing herself back from Bennett's rock-hard arm, Salisa tried to regain her composure. She felt her cheeks grow hot, but when she looked at Bennett, he was chuckling.

"I'm sorry, Bennett," she said, losing her momentary embarrassment.

He smoothed the few drops of tea that had splattered onto his dark blue university sweatshirt. "That's okay, Salisa." Surveying the tea cups, he said, "Oh! Your tea got spilled!" His concern was comic. "Here, take mine. No, really, I insist."

Giving into laughter, Salisa took both cups and set them on the nightstand. Repositioning her back against the wall, Salisa took a deep breath. "Though I like to give you a hard time, Bennett, I'm glad you're here."

"Really? Why?"

Salisa sighed again. She wasn't stalling for time but was trying to think of an honest answer. "Though I never thought I'd say it, spending a week in relative isolation in Russia has given me a new appreciation for familiarity. It's just good to see someone from the 'old life.' Know what I mean?"

Bennett nodded. "And it's good to be with someone who knows what kind of things we're experiencing here. Know what I mean?" he mimicked.

Salisa smiled and then bit her lip. "So, who are we going to be after this year in England? Social misfits? Anglo-Americans in limbo land?"

Bennett laughed as he shook his head. "All I know is that life will never be the same. Once you get another culture into your system, I don't think you can ever be a thorough-bred American again." This thought brought a smile to Bennett's face.

"It is kind of nice, isn't it?" asked Salisa softly. "But the only bad thing about it is that no one will be able to understand once we're home. It will be like waking up from a dream that no one else had. Everything will be like it was when we left, except that we'll have all these incredible memories to draw on for the rest of our lives."

"Salisa, I'll be able to understand," Bennett gently reminded her. "It's like you said. *We* will have the same kinds of memories. At least we'll have each other to talk to."

Though Salisa didn't say so aloud, she hadn't planned on spending much time with Bennett once this year was over. But then she quickly realized she hadn't planned on spending any time with him in England, either, and here he was chatting with her in her room. And she was enjoying his company! This thought sobered her up. All to herself, she quietly renewed her determination not to get too buddy-buddy with Bennett.

Bennett responded to her serious quietness. "Hey," he inquired gently. "Did I say something wrong?"

"Of course not," Salisa assured him. Bennett didn't have to know that he was overstepping the boundaries she had drawn around herself. To divert his train of thought, she suddenly began studying him intently.

"I was just trying to remember what your hair was like before Christmas. It's a lot shorter than when you left for home, isn't it?" Bennett studied Salisa with narrowed eyes. She could tell that he was skeptical of her sudden interest in his hair, but she knew he was too nice to question her about it.

Giving in, he rubbed the top of his head with his palm. "It *is* a lot shorter," he said. "Hazel cut it. She's been practicing with Ali Stromley during her Christmas break. You know Ali," Bennett suddenly remembered.

Hazel and Ali's friendship was news to Salisa. "Of course I know Ali," said Salisa. "That's how I met you. But I haven't kept in very good touch with her. I do write—about once or twice a month—but I guess it seems like longer to the person living in Pepperton."

"That's for sure," said Bennett. "That's all I heard from Hazel while I was home."

Bennett seemed to want to talk again about his relationship, and Salisa was feeling easygoing enough to let him. "So, what's up with you two?"

"Well, there's really not much to tell," said Bennett.

*Show some interest*, Salisa encouraged herself. *That's usually what he's looking for.* So she tried again. "Four weeks home? I'm sure you two covered plenty of ground."

"Why do you want to know?"

"Forget it then," said Salisa. "You're right. I really don't want to know." Though Bennett's privacy piqued her curiosity, she didn't want him thinking she was merely hungry for juicy hometown gossip.

"Listen, I'll make you a deal," Bennett offered.

"What?"

"I'll tell you about Hazel if you tell me about Nigel."

Salisa glared at him. "What's there to tell?"

"You seem to forget that Nigel and I are pretty good friends."

Salisa opened her mouth as if to say something, but then quickly pursed her lips. Bennett was probably bluffing. "Okay," she said. "You go first."

"The big news is. . .," Bennett paused for effect. "Hazel and I are on the rocks."

"That's not news!" Salisa playfully hit Bennett with her

pillow. "Anyone could figure that out! She goes home after being with you for only a few weeks in England. . .didn't you think that would put a strain on your relationship?"

"But the strain is of a serious sort now." He left it at that.

Why was Bennett being so mysterious? Though she didn't want to admit it to herself, Salisa found his teasing appealing. She sat against the corner walls behind her bed and clutched her pillow to her chest. "I'm not going to pry, Bennett," she said in a motherly, scolding tone. "If you need to talk about you and Hazel, that's fine. I'll listen. And when you're ready to hear about my travels, then I'll tell you. Just quit playing all these mind games with me. It's tiring!"

"Okay," he finally said. "I should be sad because it's breaking up between us, but I'm not. And now that I'm here," he looked around Salisa's room, "it's beginning to seem like even more of a bother. Part of me wants to quit trying to make it work. There's a whole world out there just waiting to be experienced!" Bennett's eyes were bright again.

Then his voice lowered. "You know what it's like to be torn in two different directions, don't you, Salisa?" Bennett's tone was gentle.

"Do I?" Salisa wanted to make sure she and Bennett were talking about the same thing.

"I'm facing the same decision you are now, only I don't know if Hazel will be as patient as Dale's been with you."

"Wait a minute," said Salisa, curling up a little tighter in her corner. "I don't remember telling you *anything* about my relationship back home!" Her tone was accusing.

"Remember, Hazel's been hanging around with Ali Stromley," said Bennett. "And that led to Hazel and I spending a few evenings with Ali and Ted."

Salisa felt a twinge of sorrow for the times at Ali's that she had left behind. Ali had always been great with "foursomes." Kind of like Sophie. Salisa's mind bounced from memory to memory.

"To sum up my story in a sentence," continued Bennett, "Hazel's ready for a decision. I think hanging around Ali and Ted's new place has somehow given her ideas."

"I wouldn't doubt it," Salisa mumbled.

"In fact," Bennett continued, "she's given me until our next break—when is it, March?—to make up my mind."

"Yikes! An ultimatum!" Salisa genuinely felt sorry for Bennett. The pressure of being back in Pepperton with a marriage hanging over his head was something she could relate to.

"So what are you going to do?" Salisa asked Bennett. "Do you love her enough to go along with her terms?"

Bennett was smiling, but his head was tilted toward his lap. When he looked at Salisa, his eyes were misty. "I thought I loved her," he said. "In some ways. . .all the initial ways at least. Our families have so much in common. And I have some really good memories." He swallowed. "But you can't love someone who demands that you be someone other than who you are."

Salisa moved in toward him. "And that's what she's asking you to do?" Despite her intentions to be guarded, Salisa wanted to touch his arm to show that she understood. But she didn't.

Salisa let some silence pass between them. "Well, if it's any consolation," she said abruptly, "I've come to the conclusion that I've sat on the fence long enough. I don't know what or who is the right answer for me, but I do know that it's time to be honest with Dale. . .and with myself. I think we need to officially break up."

"But Dale isn't asking you to forget all your dreams, is he?" Bennett asked. "From what I know of him, it seems like he's been really gracious. I don't know if I could wait as long for someone as he's been waiting for you."

"You would if you thought it was the right person."

Salisa was shocked by her own statement. When Bennett

gave her a quizzical look, she shrugged and said, "I don't know where that came from either. I think I read too many Shakespearean romances during break." But deep down, Salisa knew that she longed for the kind of love that was swift but sure, no agonizing compromises or a sense that she was settling for what was expected. But, even as she longed for it, she didn't think it existed.

"So, what about Nigel?" Bennett asked, hesitating a little. "Is there a place for him in the picture?"

Salisa grimaced. "Your guess is as good as mine." She still wasn't sure what Bennett knew, or didn't know, about her and Nigel's growing friendship. Then she smiled. "But it would be handy, wouldn't it?"

Bennett looked confused.

"Think about it. If I married someone like Nigel, I wouldn't have to face Dale when I went home. And marrying a missionary is kind of like marrying a minister's son, wouldn't you say? It's a way out of Pepperton while still fulfilling everyone's expectations. Well, not everyone's," Salisa added, thinking momentarily of Dale and Ali.

Bennett shook his head. "Salisa," he said, almost incredulously. "You're not thinking straight. Those aren't good reasons to get married. Tell me you're not being serious."

"I won't lie and say the idea never crossed my mind," said Salisa. "But I don't think I could do it. . .marry for the wrong reasons, that is. If I can muster up enough courage to break up with Dale, then I certainly wouldn't want to fall into the same trap again."

Salisa took a good hard look at Bennett. He was staring straight ahead again, as if deep in thought. She looked at the clock on her nightstand, and then back at Bennett. She didn't have the energy for any more deep questions and answers. And she had already opened up to Bennett more than she ever thought she would.

"Bennett, can I get you another cup of tea before you

leave?" This was another one of the get-straight-to-the-point lines she'd learned from Sophie. "I don't want you to have to walk home across town in the middle of the night. I'm not kicking you out or anything. . .just being concerned for your safety."

If Bennett was offended, he didn't show it. But Salisa hadn't been prepared for his "Sure, I'll have a cup." When she looked at him as if to verify his answer, he said in his sweetest tone, "And I'll have some cream from the windowsill."

Lest her offer sound insincere, Salisa got up to make some tea. When she went to the sill to get the cream, Salisa shivered. Pulling the curtain back let in a noticeable waft of icy air.

"It's getting messy out there," Salisa said, peering down into St. Anne's lighted courtyard. "And it's snowing! Are you sure you want a cup of tea?"

"You promised!"

"That's an evil grin if I ever saw one, Bennett Havana. And if you get caught in a snowdrift on the way home tonight, don't say I didn't try to send you home before the weather got worse."

"What difference will ten more minutes make?"

"It takes at least three for the kettle to boil," said Salisa. "That leaves you seven to drink it." She looked up to make sure Bennett knew she was kidding, and she was surprised to see him staring intently at her, with a calm smile gently curving the corners of his lips.

Within the predicted three minutes, Salisa's kettle began to whistle. As she poured the hot water into two cups, a nearby branch sounded like it was scraping the wall near her window. Salisa and Bennett looked at each other with wide eyes, but then turned up toward the shaded light bulb. It flickered a few times and then went out completely.

"Bennett!" Salisa screamed involuntarily. Though she

didn't want to admit it, she was a little scared. Bennett calmly asked if she had any candles, and in a few minutes they had found them and had them lit. They looked at each other and around the room, watching the strange shadows the tiny flames were creating.

Salisa was the first to speak. "I feel like this night is turning into a marathon. First you make me laugh, and then we bring up all this sticky stuff from home, and now we're sitting through a power outage."

"Never a dull moment around you, Salisa," Bennett said cheerily.

"That's one thing I haven't changed my mind about," replied Salisa.

"What's that?"

"You are such a crazy optimist!"

"I'm insulted!" Bennett pretended. He reached for his coat. "Really, Salisa, I should go. You asked me to leave a little while ago, and like you predicted, the weather's only getting worse. It's now or never." He had his coat on before Salisa could figure out how she wanted to respond.

"But. . .I'd rather you stick around for just a little longer now," she said as confidently as she could. "I'm not scared, but I really wouldn't mind some company. Just for a little while. . .until the wind dies down. It probably will soon." She jumped up and ran to the window. "I think it is already! Here, finish your tea."

Bennett sat down slowly as if he'd planned Salisa's short speech himself. "You'd make a lousy weatherman, Salisa. First it's a blizzard that's getting worse by the second and then it's clearing up just as fast—"

"I know," she laughed. "I wouldn't be able to make up my mind. But I do know that I wouldn't mind if you stayed just a little bit longer. Just until—"

"I know, I know," laughed Bennett. "Just until the wind dies down."

"Not because I'm scared."

"Not because you're scared," Bennett obliged her.

They talked until the wee hours of the morning.

# eleven

As Salisa worked on her CU plans during the next few days, her mind kept drifting back to Bennett's visit. What bothered her most about it was not the fact that he had left at five-fifteen in the morning, for he had been a perfect gentleman. What bothered her was how much fun the night had been. Despite Salisa's tiredness, Bennett had made her laugh and laugh.

They had also had a few more serious discussions. Bennett had been fascinated by all the sights she had seen in Russia, and he had liked hearing about the different houses and food traditions that she had encountered when staying with friends in the other parts of Great Britain. Bennett was especially interested in her time in Ireland "since I know Nigel," Bennett had said.

Salisa relished the retelling of her Ireland stories. She and Nigel had visited a city-wide young peoples' rally one night, and Salisa had even been asked to pray. "It's kind of like the time you opened up the AQ meeting at St. Oswald's," she explained to Bennett. Salisa went on to tell Bennett how respected Nigel was among his peers in Belfast, just like at Abingdon.

"Nigel's a great guy, isn't he Salisa?" Bennett had asked, with minor variations, more than once. And he had seemed more than casually interested in her response. Salisa tried to get by with a simple "yes" each time Bennett asked the rhetorical question, supposing that maybe Nigel had hinted to Bennett that he enjoyed Salisa's company. Maybe Bennett was looking out for his friend, trying to discover exactly where Salisa stood on the friendship.

But Salisa herself didn't even know where she stood with the friendship. Nor did she see the need to analyze it or define it to death. Until Nigel broached the subject, she was going to assume everything was okay. Her first priority had to be making the clean break with Dale. And her second would be making the most of her remaining time in Abingdon.

When Salisa had told Bennett about the places she planned to visit in Europe during her next break, Bennett had looked wistful. "I'd like to go there someday," he had said. But it was clear that he wasn't able to take advantage of their Easter holidays because of other obligations.

Salisa had encouraged Bennett to be honest with Hazel. "Just say it like it is, as gently as you can," she had advised him. Talking it through with Salisa seemed to solidify for Bennett the idea of a complete breakup. Bennett's resolve, in turn, helped Salisa feel more comfortable about her own plans to walk away from the five-year relationship with Dale. But, unlike Bennett, Salisa didn't want to handle things person-to-person; she opted to try a series of letters. By the end of the night, they knew each other's strategies backward and forward.

This building sense of intimacy bothered Salisa more than anything else. She waited for her CU jobs to pull her mind away from Bennett and home and, thankfully, she had invited some of St. Anne's Bible study leaders to return early so they could help with the planning. She hadn't realized how much she had missed these warm, caring young women until they were sitting on her floor with her, laughing and eating toasties with extra cheese.

Salisa happened to be alone one afternoon, stapling a batch of Bible study guides, when she heard a high-pitched voice go by outside her door.

"And hallo to you too, Sarah! I'll be round for tea once

I've unpacked me bags a bit."

Salisa jumped up and opened the door. "Sophie!"

The dark-headed girl dropped her bags, turned around instinctively, and ran to give her friend a hug.

"So you made it out of London all right, I see," she said, looking Salisa up and down. "Although you look a little on the thin side. Did you not like all the different foods you tried on your travels?"

"I ate what I could identify," Salisa answered. "Here, let me help you. The sooner you're moved in, the sooner you can help me with a few CU dilemmas. What do you do when more girls sign up for Bible studies than you have leaders for?"

Sophie came up alongside her friend. "And I'm going to need lots of help with Shakespeare," she said breathlessly. Her small size made her overstuffed bags a challenge to transport down the narrow hall. "Jo Brand. . .you know, the one who's playin' Hermia in the play? She rang me up to tell me she can't do it! Her studies are sufferin' too much."

"Oh, no," Salisa gasped. Hermia was one of the two leading female roles in *A Midsummer Night's Dream*. "What are you going to do?"

"How's your British accent?" Sophie said sarcastically.

"You're kidding, I hope."

"I hope I'm kiddin'," said Sophie, plopping down on her bed when they entered her room. "But you'll probably be the one who has to spend extra time with whoever we find to do it."

"I should be able to," answered Salisa. "If you help me get these Bible study schedules figured out before everyone moves back in. So many people are interested all of a sudden."

"You're absolutely right," said Sophie, plopping her bags on the floor just inside the doorway. "I think Nigel was doing an excellent job at the AQ meetings toward the end of last term. He really has a gentle way of challengin' people to get their lives straight with God, don't you think?"

"Absolutely." Salisa suspected that Sophie would postpone unpacking for as long as possible, so she was helping her get as many bags as she could out of the line of traffic.

"Speakin' of Nigel," Sophie continued, "have you seen him around yet? It would be fun to get together with him and Bennett to see how everyone's break went."

Salisa's stomach did a double flip-flop. She didn't know why—or for whom. All she knew was that she *had* been looking forward to seeing Nigel, but now the feeling wasn't so strong. And would it be weird to see Bennett after their all-night discussion in her room?

"Salisa? You have a funny look on your face. What's up?"

Salisa thought fast. "I was just thinking that maybe we should wait a few weeks or so. . .just to give everyone a chance to settle in." *And myself a chance to figure out what's going on in my own head!* Salisa added in her thoughts.

To Salisa's relief, Sophie agreed. "I suppose you're right," she said, rolling up shirts from her suitcase and sticking them back into drawers. "But let's not wait too long." On impulse, she threw one of her rolled-up shirts at Salisa, hitting her right in the face. "It took you most of last term to figure out that men like Bennett and Nigel could be fun to have around," she said laughing and rolling up another one. "And I'm not in the mood to retrain you!"

Salisa picked up the first shirt and threw it back with a vengeance. She'd forgotten how much fun Sophie could be! The two tossed other items of clothing back and forth for a few minutes, still laughing and making Sophie's room even messier. Salisa gathered an armful and ran over to Sophie, tackled her, and then sat on her.

"Say, 'uncle,' Barnes!"

"What?" Sophie gasped and laughed as Salisa lightly bounced on top of her.

"Oh, that's right. I forgot. You probably don't know what that means. So I'll give you a break." The minute she released Sophie, Salisa ran out the open door and pulled it closed behind her. Sophie ran up to the door and tugged from inside a few times, but then gave up.

"Now, you just stay put and get that room cleaned up," Salisa shouted through the door good naturedly. "You're the last one to come back from Christmas, and if I know you, you won't unpack until it's time to get ready to go home for Easter!"

"You're a mean friend," Sophie called back from what must have been a far corner of her room. "But I'll probably thank you tomorrow for not draggin' me down to the snack bar for a toastie. Of course, I could be persuaded should you care to ask me—"

"Can't," said Salisa, opening Sophie's door a few inches and poking her head in. "I have work to do. And so do you. How about I come back for tea? Say around ten?"

Sophie was unraveling what looked like all kinds of striped socks tied together and knotted in a ball. "It's the least you can do," she said, giving Salisa her best fake pout. "We have lots of catchin' up to do."

Salisa gave her a wink as a goodbye. "See you then, Soph."

It was great to be with Sophie again. Reunions with good friends were sweet and exhilarating. But then the thought came: Would she feel the same way when she saw Nigel?

The first AQ meeting of the new term was packed. Salisa and Sophie had arrived late because Sophie had insisted on finding the perfect tiara for one of the fairies in her play and then bringing it all the way back to St. Anne's so it didn't get wet or lost or anything else equally tragic. Salisa had trailed along because she wanted to spend a rare few hours with Sophie, but she thought all the extra walking was ridiculous.

"Now really, Sophie," Salisa continued to lecture as they entered St. Oswald's side door. "Was it absolutely necessary that we return the tiara to your room *before* the meeting? We've already missed half of it!" They found a few empty folding chairs in the back and didn't disrupt too many people around them with the taking off of their coats, scarves, and gloves.

Salisa didn't want to admit it but, in a way, she was glad they were late. Sophie had eliminated the possibility that she would run into either Bennett or Nigel before the meeting. Neither one had crossed her path during the first few weeks of the term and this way she would have a chance to watch Nigel up on the church's platform for a good half hour before having to talk with him. Salisa also figured that she'd probably be able to find Bennett in the crowds before he spotted her. Seeing them without their seeing her would help Salisa feel prepared for the initial post-holiday meetings.

Nigel was well into his message when Salisa got situated in her seat and began studying him. He looked the same, and Salisa felt somewhat proud of him as he spoke with his typical conviction and wisdom. She was watching him gesture, holding the Bible in one hand and holding the other out to the audience, when, out of the corner of her eye, she saw Sophie turn around. She began waving to someone behind her.

"Sure, sit over here," she heard Sophie whisper not very softly. "There's an extra chair over by Salisa." Salisa tried to keep her attention focused on Nigel, but it became difficult when a large man walked through their row, pressing against people's legs and dodging their toes. She felt a familiarity and looked up to verify what her senses had suggested. Bennett sat down next to her and gave her one of his million-dollar smiles.

"Hi, Salisa," was all he said. And then he leaned forward

and began taking off his jacket. The rows of chairs didn't have very much room between them, and Bennett was soon stuck because he couldn't lean forward enough to pull his arms out of his sleeves. Salisa instinctively helped Bennett by pulling backward on his hood and collar.

"Thanks, Salisa," Bennett said, taking the coat from her.

"No problem," she answered, returning her attention to Nigel. For some strange reason, Salisa was suddenly conscious of her hair. She tried to remember if she had pulled it up in one of those side twists that Nigel's mother had said accentuated her high cheekbones. Salisa lifted her left hand to scratch a pretend itch on her ear, planning to check for the barrette that she hoped would be there. It was.

On the way back down to her side, Salisa's hand momentarily hit Bennett's leg. The chairs were so close that it was hard to avoid each other completely.

"Sorry, Bennett," she whispered. She had pulled her hand away as quickly as she could, but not before her fingertips registered the solidness of Bennett's leg.

"No problem, Salisa," Bennett said, lightly putting his hand on her leg and squeezing her knee. "There. We're even." He removed his hand as quickly as it had descended.

Salisa thought she felt her face flush a little and hoped that it was only her imagination. She immediately looked up and tried to resume interest in what Nigel was saying.

"I understand some of the colleges have their own 'welcome-back' get-togethers going on this evening," he was saying, "so I won't be keeping you as late as usual. Please carry on with the spirit of the evening. Grab a guitar and pray and just enjoy the spirit of the fellowship of Christ." There was a brief closing prayer, and the meeting was over.

Nigel must have spotted Bennett and Sophie and Salisa while he was speaking because as soon as the group began to disperse, he found the straightest path he could—through various groups of people—and reached them before they had a chance to get into a conversation themselves.

"Just the people I was looking for!" Nigel was clearly glad to see Sophie and Salisa. He gave each of them a fatherly pat on the shoulder and then looked directly at Bennett.

"How'd the meeting go, Bennett? Were the vicars responsive to involving Chadwick in the first part of the week rather than the latter?"

"I can tell you all about it later," Bennett said, giving Nigel a playful punch in the arm. "The meeting went just as you hoped. The vicars said they'd take whatever manpower Chadwick was willing to donate for their fundraiser. They'll be sending you a copy of the itinerary once they have it all drawn up."

Bennett turned toward the women. "That's why I was late. Somebody scheduled Chadwick's CU to be two different places at the same time!"

"So what's your excuse?" Nigel asked Sophie and Salisa. He looked so serious, almost upset, that for a few seconds, Salisa wasn't sure whether he was kidding or not.

"It's not as spiritual as Bennett's," Sophie muttered. But then she quickly brightened. "But look at it this way. By being late, we got to sit with Bennett! With this many people, it's a wonder we've all found each other."

"Good point." Nigel turned to glance around the room. "It looks like things are pretty well under control. It's not my turn to lock up." He turned back toward his friends and brushed his hands back and forth a few times. "Let's go have some tea!" he said abruptly. "Just the four of us."

Sophie jumped a few inches in the air and clapped her hands. "Excellent idea!" she said. "I was waiting for someone to ask. But I think it's the men's turn to walk over to St. Anne's. And besides, Salisa and I have done plenty of walkin' for one day." She looked to Salisa to confirm her suggestion.

Salisa had been unusually quiet up to this point, but she simply couldn't think of anything to say. With all three of her friends looking at her, however, she realized that she was going to have to loosen up or one of them—probably Sophie—would start asking questions.

"Great idea, Soph," Salisa said. But her voice was unnatural. To compensate, she reminded herself that these were friends. There was no need to be so nervous. Salisa forced herself to be more animated.

"I have an idea," she offered, consciously smiling at no one in particular. "Why don't we walk toward St. Anne's via High Street. . .the way Nigel kept asking us to try last year? Remember? We never did. Every time we were together, we always ended up taking Sophie's favorite route back and forth through town."

"Hey! That's right,"agreed Nigel. "I forgot about that. Why didit always work out that way?"

"Because Bennett usually agreed with me," Sophie said coyly, tipping her head toward Bennett.

"Great minds think alike," joked Bennett.

"Well, then, it's settled," said Salisa, ready to get a breath of fresh air. The sooner they were started on this walk, the sooner she could curl up in her bed with a hot water bottle on her sore, tired calf muscles. It wasn't that she wanted the night to be over, in fact, she was happy with the way the evening was turning out. Walking with Nigel and Bennett in the dark would be a way to catch up on holiday news without having to sit through any deep, eyeball-to-eyeball discussions. And Sophie would keep things lively.

But Sophie began to keep things too lively for Salisa's liking. They were hardly out of the church when Sophie locked arms with Bennett and began reminding him of all the fun times they had had last term. She brought up some of the American jokes Bennett had taught her and reported on how they had succeeded—or not succeeded—with her all-British family back home. Salisa thought Sophie was getting a little too giddy and silly, but she kept hearing Bennett's deep belly laugh, which indicated that he must have been enjoying her company.

Since the sidewalk was only wide enough for two people, and Sophie had firmly attached herself to Bennett, that left Salisa to walk in front with Nigel. Nigel began telling Salisa about all the AQ messages he had planned for the upcoming term, but he stopped talking long enough for Salisa to hear Bennett say, "It was good to be home, but I've sure missed my British friends." Then she heard Sophie squeal and speculated that Bennett must have put his arm around her shoulder and pulled her head in toward his chest, giving her one of his affectionate "Dutch rubs" with the knuckles of his free hand. She'd see him do it to some of his male friends before, but never to a woman.

Salisa wanted to turn around to watch the fun Bennett and Sophie seemed to be having but instead, she kept up the front that indicated interest in Nigel's monologue. Bennett and Sophie continued their talking and joking in earnest but after a while, they settled into silence.

"I haven't had the chance to thank you again for the really nice time I had in Ireland," Salisa began, interrupting Nigel's discourse on the discipleship talk that he planned to give that May. "I. . .I just wanted to say that before I forgot."

Nigel was surprised by the abrupt change of subject, but the mention of Salisa's visit appeared to spark fond memories in him. Nigel looked at her for a moment, and then said, "It was great to have you. I think I enjoyed your visit even more than I enjoyed putting all these messages together."

Salisa knew he intended the comparison to be a compliment. "You were the perfect host," she returned. Sophie and Bennett were still quiet, and for some reason, Salisa

ound herself wanting to prove that she and Nigel had
chieved as good a time in Ireland as Sophie and Bennett
were having on their arm-in-arm stroll. They just didn't need
o be as rowdy.

"It was easy to be the perfect host when you were the
erfect guest," Nigel returned, borrowing Salisa's original
ompliment to him.

"No," she said, smiling and shaking her head. "I just sat
ack and enjoyed that wonderful guest room, all the great
ood your mother cooked, and your fine chauffeuring ser-
ice all around Belfast." Salisa looked behind her, pretend-
ng to just realize that Sophie and Bennett had been quiet
or a while. True to Salisa's expectations, they were listen-
ng.

"Don't let Nigel fool you," she said, smiling at Bennett
nd Sophie behind her. "He's as charming a host as they
ome."

Salisa couldn't be sure, but she thought Nigel was begin-
ing to blush. "Salisa, really. You're making too much of it.
t was just fun to have you around—your enthusiasm, your
willingness to sit and let my mother teach you how to do
er favorite kind of needlepoint, the way you helped us with
ome of the work around the house." Now it was Nigel's
urn to turn around and talk to Sophie and Bennett.

"Salisa could have stayed the whole five weeks' worth of
oliday break with us if she wanted," he said.

"Now, aren't you glad I talked you into staying at least a
week in Ireland?" Sophie questioned in her most authorita-
ive voice.

"Sounds like it was a good move, Soph," Bennett added.
And then Bennett and Sophie resumed their bantering by
omparing how often different predictions they made came
rue.

By this time, they were nearing the cobblestoned High
Street. Salisa had been here only once before and that had

been during the daytime. It had been quaint then, but now it was almost magical. A row of narrow homes joined each other in salute to the cathedral directly across the river from them, and since they were at the point where the river bottom was rockiest, the four friends heard the whoosh of rushing water. Salisa couldn't decide whether to turn toward the sounds and smells of the water, with the lighted cathedral wall towering above it, or toward the homes on her right, where warm lamps glowed from behind delicate lace curtains, allowing just enough of a peek inside to see the coziness of furniture and fancy wallpaper and small brick fireplaces.

Nigel leaned over and whispered in Salisa's ear. "I'd like to bring you back here sometime. . .just the two of us. Those two are kind of ruining it for me." Sophie and Bennett were still talking loudly behind them.

Salisa merely smiled in response. Somehow, quietness didn't seem to be the missing ingredient on this beautiful late-night walk. But Salisa couldn't put her finger on what she sensed was lacking.

The end of High Street was close to the gravel path that led up to St. Anne's. Here, the foursome decided to part ways.

"Are you sure you don't want to come up for some tea?" pleaded Sophie. "That was part of the plan, you know. Nigel, I think it was your idea."

"But I didn't realize how late it would get," replied Nigel, looking at his watch as furtively as he had been ever since he remembered that he had to teach a church school class the following morning. "I really need to go over my notes a few more times." He sounded anxious.

"Well, then, Bennett can still come," Sophie proposed.

"Nah, I'll head back with Nige," said Bennett. "Thanks anyway."

There were a few quick hugs, and Salisa thought Sophie

held on to Bennett just a little too long.

As soon as they were out of earshot, Salisa said casually, "I don't remember you and Bennett ever laughing so hard before. You two must have really missed each other."

Sophie was all wound up. "It was just so much fun tonight," she said, her eyes still dancing with the excitement of the evening. She was half skipping and half walking. "I didn't know Bennett could be so much fun."

*Neither did I*, thought Salisa. And was Bennett like this with every woman he met, whether British or American? Did he warm up to them, make them laugh, and then chalk up another conquest for his list of female admirers?

Her initial distrust of him was returning. And then an even stranger thought came to Salisa: What if Bennett was starting to care for Sophie in the same way that she and Nigel were getting close? Had Bennett tried to get to know Salisa better that night of the snowstorm in an effort to build a bridge to Sophie?

With these questions running through her mind, Salisa was suddenly glad that, following an interesting night such as the one they had just had, Sophie could amuse herself by repeating snatches of conversations and laughing at the funny things she or somebody else had said. Salisa could enjoy Sophie's company without having to muster the effort to return the dialogue.

But sometimes Sophie drew her in anyway. "And then do you know what Bennett said?" Sophie was asking Salisa.

"No, what?"

"That things weren't going so well with that woman named Hazel at home and that he was hopin' to spend more time with people like us this term."

"That's interesting," Salisa said with next to no emotion in her voice. "What else did he have to say?"

But Sophie couldn't really think of anything that she hadn't already talked about several times over. So she asked Salisa,

"What were you and Nigel talkin' about all night? You both seemed to have had a good time when you visited him in Ireland."

Salisa told her about a few of their more adventurous nights in Belfast, just stopping short of the details that led to their heart-to-heart talk on the couch. But Salisa had told enough to fuel Sophie's imagination.

"See?" Sophie said, slipping her arm into Salisa's as they walked up the stairs toward St. Anne's. "What'd I tell you? It's happenin'."

But Salisa wasn't sure what was happening. And she didn't want to ask Sophie for her interpretation of "it," which would only lead to more exhausting analyses and giddy expectations.

"It's late, Soph," Salisa said as soon as they reached her room. "I'm going to fill a hot water bottle and call it a night."

"No late-night toasties?" Sophie implored.

"Let's start earlier tomorrow night."

Sophie accepted the offer and went off humming toward her room. Salisa got ready for bed, trying hard to figure out why she was so sad.

## twelve

"I really think you should go," said Maureen. "I would like for a few more older Americans to be going and, besides, it will take your mind off the situation."

Salisa had stopped in for a visit, claiming that she had simply been craving coffee and needed a "quick fix." But Maureen had sensed that Salisa had more than coffee on her mind. Finally, Salisa had spilled a few details of her recent afternoons with Nigel in the CU office. Nigel had asked her to help him put together a new Bible study series and while he was acting somewhat "interested," Salisa didn't want to make any assumptions. She also didn't want to ignore the situation, having heard Sophie's warning not to let friendships "simmer" in silence until they erupted at the official end of the CU term in mid-June.

"I just don't know how to interpret British men," she had told Maureen. "But you must. After all, you married one."

But Maureen didn't know Nigel that well and, as a result, was hesitant to offer her opinions. "I'm sure it will work itself out," she consoled. "And it sounds like you're spending plenty of time with other friends, too. That's always the safe thing to do."

Salisa still hadn't figured out what, if anything, was happening between Bennett and Sophie. And she didn't want to bring it up because she knew Sophie would see her questions as encouragement. So she felt stuck, not being able to move forward toward solving what was perplexing her.

"By the way you're gulping that coffee, I think what you need is a little time with your fellow citizens," Maureen continued her sales pitch. "And you're such a hard worker.

You need some time for a little rest and relaxation."

"But a whole weekend?" Salisa asked. "I never saw that on the schedule of events you gave me at the beginning of the year."

"We just got the deal on the ski lodge last week," Maureen replied. "And so far, I've been able to get almost all of the forty undergraduate Americans here to go. Won't you consider it? Remember, cross-country skiing is great exercise!"

"Maureen," Salisa said, offering her cup for a refill. "With all the hiking I do back and forth from St. Anne's into town, I'm having a hard enough time as it is keeping weight on!"

"But you're still liking it?" Maureen queried.

"'Like' doesn't begin to cover it," Salisa replied. "But I can't figure out what has made me want a cup of coffee all of a sudden. Maybe I am missing home more than I thought."

"Then it's settled," said Maureen. "Part of the American outings I arrange involve good ol' American food. We'll be making burgers and hot dogs quite a bit up at the lodge. And nice fluffy American pancakes for breakfast."

This last bit of bait was hard to resist. "I suppose it wouldn't hurt for me to get to know some of the Americans here a little better," suggested Salisa. "I've been so busy trying to get to know Brits that I can invite to the CU . . .maybe there are some Americans who might like to get involved too.

Having come up with a sensible reason for spending a weekend with Americans, Salisa agreed to do so.


Bennett Havana turned out to be another one of Maureen's last-minute invitees. Salisa was taken aback for a moment when, shortly after arriving at their lodge in the low, snowy Pennine Alps, she saw Bennett jump out of the last van of the convoy. She watched as he helped unload the cargo, his broad shoulders and stocking-capped head sticking up a full half-foot above everyone else's. When he glanced to the lodge's doorway, where Salisa was standing, Salisa quickly covered her surprised reaction with a wave.

"Hi, Bennett! Long time, no see!"

He walked over, surprised as she was. "I didn't know you were coming on this trip," was all he could say. Salisa saw a few dimples begin to form in his cold-reddened face.

"It's good to see you again," Salisa responded. And she meant it. A few faint memories from the night they had stayed up talking started to creep in around the edges of her consciousness. Salisa pushed them away, but she couldn't quite pull herself away from staring at Bennett. He looked so muscular and healthy.

"It's great to see you too, Salisa," Bennett said. "Maybe we'll have some more time to sit and catch up on each other's news." His warm breath was making small clouds in front of his face.

"Sure," replied Salisa. A part of her was craving the idea of being alone with Bennett again, but she didn't want to admit this to herself, let alone Bennett.

"I have some English books I'm trying to get through this weekend," she pointed out, "but I'll probably be reading them by the big fireplace in the main lobby." Salisa used her thumb to point behind her. "You should see it. It's magnificent." She hoped Bennett was interested in interior architecture.

Bennett's warm smile seemed to indicate that he'd see her there. "I've got to go help unload now," he said. "But maybe I'll see you later."

Salisa spent the rest of the afternoon skiing and meeting new people, working up an appetite, and then eating too many hamburgers and hot dogs. As soon as the dishes were done, she claimed a spot on the hearth of the stone fireplace that spanned a full side of the lodge's main room. She told herself that she didn't care whether Bennett showed up or not. She had brought plenty along to read, and she hadn't anticipated his being there anyway. But deep down, she wanted to tease Bennett again, to laugh with him like they had that cold snowy night in her room at St. Anne's.

Some of the group had gone outside to ice skate and a few were in other rooms, playing games. But for the most part, the lodge was quiet. The silence, combined with the afternoon's exercise and the heavy solidness she now felt in her stomach, was making Salisa drowsy. She let her eyes close just for a minute.

Salisa let herself remember the feel of the cold, wet flecks of blowing snow that had chapped her cheeks that afternoon. Then, her body had felt cold and damp, and now, she was warm. Deliciously warm. Almost too warm.

"Salisa," a low voice said behind her. Before she could open her eyes, a pair of hands gently pulled her in a backward direction. "You're going to get sparks in your hair if you go to sleep like that." It was Bennett.

"Oh, hi, Bennett," Salisa said sleepily. The warmth of the fire had worked as a tranquilizer.

Bennett, whose cheeks were burnished from the cold weather that afternoon, turned his back toward the fire and sat down beside her.

Salisa tried to think of something to say, but her mind was too tired. Again, she felt herself drifting into sleep. But something seemed to stir her, and Salisa tried to open her eyes. A face was in front of her. . .Bennett's face. . .and he had his eyes closed and was moving closer. Salisa tried to speak, but no sound came out. She felt like she was floating and let herself fall away from the advancing face. But something gently lifted the back of her head as something soft touched her lips.

The scene was strange enough to be a dream. She pinched herself—a favorite trick from childhood—and this time she felt her eyelids flutter open again. Only this time, her eyelids were heavy and her body felt stiff. She propped herself up from where she must have fallen asleep.

When she looked at the chair beside her, she saw Bennett sleeping. He was sitting up but was slumped over, his head resting in a cupped hand and his elbow firmly planted on the armrest. He was breathing softly, and Salisa watched his red flannel shirt move slightly with each deep breath. His hair was curling, and his cheeks still had a glow from the warmth of the fire.

Salisa walked over to him. Bennett must have sensed her shadow because he opened his eyes. "Salisa?" he said softly. "Are you awake?"

"For now," Salisa said, sitting back down on the hearth. "I must have fallen asleep. . .at some point at least." Still somewhat drowsy, Salisa didn't know which hearth memories were dreams and which might have actually happened. "Why are you still up?" she asked Bennett.

Bennett sat straight up and tried to look awake. "I just wanted to make sure you didn't burn yourself," he said.

"A lot of good you could have done—being asleep!" kidded Salisa. Bennett gave her a tired smile. Now he was the drowsy one. Salisa watched him pull an imaginary blanket up to his chin. The embers in the fire were low by now and Salisa was beginning to feel the chill creeping toward her from the rest of the room.

"Bennett?" she tried again, this time more softly. No response. He looked almost angelic, all curled up in the high-backed Victorian chair. Though his large frame was spilling out over the armrests—he had turned sideways and was letting his feet dangle near the floor—he seemed like a child to Salisa. His soft-looking lips parted slightly as he breathed and his expression was one of innocence and trust.

She stood staring at him for a moment. He looked, well, cuddly. Salisa couldn't resist touching him once, on the cheek. When she stretched out her hand to do so, she let one finger glide through a few of his waves, then down the side of his face to where a sideburn would have been, and then across his cheek to his lips. His skin was so soft! Bennett stirred, but he didn't wake up. Salisa quickly gathered the blanket she had brought with her to the hearth and dashed upstairs.

As she quietly slipped into bed a few minutes later, Salisa couldn't forget how vulnerable Bennett had looked. But her tender feelings and actions toward Bennett scared Salisa, and suddenly, she was glad they had both fallen asleep.

"Hey! Do you own stock in this fireplace or what?" joked Bennett the following night when he spotted Salisa. His cheeks were even ruddier from a full day's worth of skiing. He stood in front of the fire and rubbed his hands together, obviously trying to warm them up.

Salisa had wanted to finish a few more chapters before she joined the others on the ice rink, but the woodsy smell of Bennett made her want to close her books and dash upstairs, just as she had done the night before. Bennett's extreme masculinity was starting to distract her.

But instead of running, Salisa chose a middle ground alternative. "I *was* here first." Salisa herself was surprised at the teasing tone that was creeping into her voice. Yet it felt natural and, after the snowball fight Bennett had initiated with her that afternoon, it seemed perfectly appropriate.

"And now you've completely ruined my concentration."

Her false aloofness was amusing Bennett. So he pushed her farther. "You're too studious, Salisa. You need to relax and have fun once in a while."

"I have plenty of fun and excitement in my life, Bennett Havana. You just don't always catch me doing it."

"I did finally catch you in action," returned Bennett. "I saw a side of you today that I knew was lurking in you since the day I met you on the train ride up to Abingdon. And next time, I'll know better. I won't start a snowball fight with someone who happened to be the all-star pitcher on her college softball team!"

"My pitching days hardly protected me, though," said Salisa. "How did you know I was okay when you left me there, lying in the snow this afternoon? For all you knew, I could have been sick, or had a concussion."

The only reply Salisa got from Bennett was a hearty "Ha! You?" He threw his head back for one more satisfied laugh. "You proved to me that snow alone isn't enough to keep you down. My only chance for getting away was to throw you over my shoulders and twirl you around until you were so dizzy you couldn't stand up for a few minutes. Then I took off."

"But some strain of courage made you come back," Salisa said softly. "How do you know I don't have a bucket of snow waiting around the corner, ready to dump on your head?"

"It wouldn't surprise me if you did, Salisa."

Salisa took this as a compliment.

"Besides," continued Bennett, "I think you've had enough for one night. Look at this wet head." Bennett slowly lifted his hand and ran his fingers through a few of her loose curls. Almost instinctively, Salisa turned her head toward Bennett's hand and closed her eyes. He held his fingers in the same place while she nodded slightly, like a cat who had found a favorite post to run his back against.

"That feels great," she murmured. The smell of the burning logs took Salisa away to other memories, and when she opened her eyes, she was almost startled to see Bennett. But the feel of his fingers running through her hair was foremost in her mind.

"You know what?" she said almost sleepily, but she wasn't sleepy. "No, I can't tell you." She looked shyly away, but in her heart, she wanted Bennett to pursue the matter further.

"What?" Bennett obliged her, following her nonverbal clues. "I know you want to tell me," he said, tousling her hair again. "Or do I hear another swirlie in the snow calling?"

"No, no!" Salisa laughed. "I was just thinking. . .well, remembering actually. . .this funny dream I had last night. I was trying to hold a conversation with you—"

"That wasn't a dream," Bennett joked. "That really happened."

"But you kept falling asleep on me."

"Now that's where you have it wrong," said Bennett. "*You* fell asleep first. I just happened to come along and move this beautiful head of hair away from the fire."

"As I was saying," Salisa went on, pretending to be annoyed at Bennett's interruption. "The dream became strange when your face filled my entire line of view." She motioned with her hands to explain her point.

"Like this?" Bennett opened his eyes wide and leaned into Salisa, causing her to lean back and laugh.

"Was I trying to scare you?" Bennett's expression told Salisa he hoped he was right. "Or threaten you with a snowball down your back?"

"No. . .at least I don't think so." Salisa thought back for a moment. Then her eyes opened a little wider in surprise. Had Salisa herself not been so surprised by the recollection, she might have weighed the impact of what she was about to say more carefully.

"I think you were trying to kiss me." She kept looking down at the floor, as if trying to believe what she had said was correct. Then she looked at Bennett with a silly grin on her face. "Can you imagine that?" she asked him. Bennett could see that that new idea was strange, even amusing to Salisa.

"Imagine that," Bennett echoed with mock amazement.

He chuckled to himself. "Salisa, where do you get all your silly ideas?"

Salisa shook her head slowly. "I don't know," she said. "Too much reading maybe? Or maybe England's dampness is starting to affect my mind somehow."

Salisa ran her fingers through her own hair. Her mind was dancing through several memories with Bennett...their talks and their recent snowball fight. "Imagine that," Salisa repeated, mostly to herself.

"You don't have to," said Bennett.

"Hmm?" Salisa wanted to understand what Bennett's alert eyes were communicating, but she couldn't quite grasp the message.

"Imagine," said Bennett softly. And before Salisa could ask any more questions, he leaned down toward her and kissed her mouth.

In that brief second that he touched her, Salisa was aware of only one sensation: something incredibly warm and soft upon her lips. Her eyes instinctively closed.

When they opened, Bennett was a foot or so away from her, looking at her with satisfaction. There was no regret or emotion, just a calm confidence.

Slowly, haltingly, Salisa whispered, "Why did you do that?" One part of Salisa was shocked and angry, but another part—the overruling part—was still spellbound by what had just happened.

"Nobody saw," was Bennett's reassuring response. "Not even you. Your eyes were closed."

Salisa opened her mouth to reply, but then stopped. She wanted to laugh at Bennett's disarming cleverness, but fought against it. How did he get her into these situations, these moods?

"So now what are we going to do?" Salisa had composed herself and her sensibilities had returned.

"What's there to do?" asked Bennett. "As far as I was

concerned, it was a harmless little kiss. Just as strange as we thought it would be."

"But it could get us into trouble," whispered Salisa, looking around furtively.

"Remember what I told you," Bennett said in a singsong voice. "Nobody saw." He tapped his index finger on her nose. "Your secret's safe with me."

"*My* secret!" Salisa whispered, glancing furtively at the snowballers who had just walked into the lodge's kitchen. "This was your doing!"

"But you dreamed it."

"But I didn't say you had to do everything I dreamed! Bennett, sometimes you don't make any sense."

"You don't either, Vrenden." Bennett got up to leave. "But that's how you charm me." With one final peck on the top of her head, Bennett walked out of the room. He didn't even look back.

Salisa's mind was a jumble of indignation and exhilaration. One part of her dredged up the earlier questions about Bennett and Sophie. Was Bennett simply an incredibly nice flirt? If so, she was mad because she had fallen for his smoothness so easily. She should have slapped him or done something equally as dramatic!

But the other part of her cherished the brief memory of his kiss. For all the times she had let Dale kiss her—and the few times she had been the one to initiate the romance— she had never experienced anything so intoxicating as Bennett's breathless "Imagine" line and the subsequent soft connection of his lips to hers.

Salisa stayed at the hearth a little longer, trying to sift through what had just happened. She looked over at the pile of books and papers she had brought down with her. There was a draft of a letter to Dale. Under that was her journal, with notes and questions that had arisen from conversations with Nigel.

And now this.

*What I need to do right now is get back to my room at St. Anne's,* Salisa resolved. *And I'm never going to trust the magic of ski-lodge hearths and late-night firelight again.* Once Salisa had worked her way back into the routines she had established in Abingdon—her CU students, her tutoring, and Sophie's play—she would be able to regain control of her life and enjoy the rest of the year.

Providing, of course, she could stay away from a particular fellow American with an uncanny ability to get under her skin.

# thirteen

"You what?" Salisa nearly yelled one fairly warm night in March when Sophie tracked her down in the dining hall. "I thought you were having rehearsals from noon until supper every day before Easter break! You don't have time for a picnic."

But Sophie was immune to Salisa's charged reaction. "I simply told Bennett I missed him. He's the one who suggested we all get together. I see you all the time, and Nigel some of the time, but Bennett never. And if I hadn't run into him in the post office, who knows how long it would have been until we did something. . .like we used to." Sophie, always eating as she waited in line for the main course, stuck a piece of buttered bread into her mouth. "Remember when we cooked them dinner here? That was so much fun!"

"So when did you tell Bennett we'd have this picnic?"

Sophie's eyes lit up. "Friday. It's supposed to be sunny and at least sixty-five degrees. And that way, we'll all have a little more time 'cause it's the weekend."

"Great idea, Soph," mumbled Salisa. Maybe life had been a little boring lately, but at least it had been predictable. But then, give someone like Sophie a free afternoon, and look what she could do with it. Salisa looked over at her friend who was eating almost as fast as the cooks were spooning food onto her plate.

"So give me the details, Soph. . .when and where. I suppose there isn't enough time to reschedule it." Since the Pennines ski trip, Salisa had felt the urge to avoid Bennett for as long as possible.

Sophie swallowed and looked proudly at Salisa. She was

determined not to let Salisa's sour spirits spoil her enthusiasm for the outing. "I was really thinking of you, Salisa," she began. "You told me once that you'd never been on a punt boat before, so that's what we decided to do. Bennett said he hadn't been punting either, so it should be fun. We'll meet at the docks at noon."

"And Nigel's going, too?"

"Bennett told me he'd ask him tonight. But he thinks Nigel is pretty free on Fridays, so it should all work out."

Nigel and Bennett were waiting by the boats when Salisa and Sophie descended the stone steps that connected Gates Street Bridge with the docks. "Hi, Nigel! Hi, Bennett!" Sophie called. Salisa watched intently for a reaction from Bennett, but there was none. Not a glimmer of excitement nor a tinge of embarrassment.

*That's good,* thought Salisa. *I'm glad he has his emotions under control because mine are certainly going to be.*

Sophie was chattering on about how much fun they were going to have, and Bennett and Salisa, on either side of Sophie, chipped in with questions and comments whenever it seemed appropriate. As they got the boat undocked and pushed into the water, the challenge of getting the punt situated was enough to capture all of their attention for a good ten to fifteen minutes. Salisa hoped they would stay on similarly superficial topics for the rest of the afternoon.

"Explain how you're steerin' the punt for the Americans," said Sophie excitedly. Before Nigel could answer, she piped, "See? Nigel's pushin' away on the pole and, dependin' on where he places it, he can steer. Isn't that right, Nigel?"

Nigel looked at Bennett and Salisa and smiled. "Of course it's physically impossible to do a good job steering a punt unless one has a navigator on board such as our dear friend Sophie."

Sophie wasn't offended by the comment and merely went

on telling the group about the history of punting and how it had come to be a part of springtime traditions around Abingdon.

Eventually, the group settled into a drowsy silence; the punt was drifting mostly on its own around the horseshoe-shaped Dell River. Nigel had punted upstream, past the English building and around the bend of the horseshoe, which was mostly wooded. He then let the punt begin to go with the current. They floated back past the docks where they had started and Salisa exclaimed, "Let's go back around the horseshoe one more time! Can we, please?" Salisa was captured by the beauty of the scenery, especially the buildings and parts of Abingdon's wooded areas that she had never seen from the vantage point of a boat before, let alone a flat-bottomed, wide-open punt. Salisa had taken the spot at the back end of the rectangular boat and Bennett was helping maintain a distance between them by staying at the front.

When they reached the part where they would turn around and head back upstream, Nigel looked at his crew. "Any takers for the punting part? It won't kill you, but it does take some strength."

Bennett stood up. "I'd like to try it, Nige," he said. "Here, show me once more how you do it." Bennett had taken off his light, tan jacket so he could move his arms better, but when he did, Salisa tried hard not to stare. Bennett had always been muscular, but now there were definitely new contours to his arms and upper back. While Salisa was gawking, Sophie spoke up for the both of them.

"Bennett! You look like you've been workin' out. Your arms are so much bigger than when we last saw you."

"You've probably never even seen my arms," Bennett replied, smiling. "It's been so cold and rainy ever since I arrived."

"No, there's been some definite growth," Sophie

continued. "Don't you think so, Salisa?"

Salisa hadn't wanted to enter this conversation, but now, thanks to Sophie, she had to. Bennett looked at her expectantly.

"Bennett's always had a nice physique," Salisa said, trying *not* to compliment Bennett any further. But a moment's reflection told her she had.

"Why, thank you," said Bennett with a glance at Salisa. Salisa turned to face the breeze so Bennett couldn't see her red face. Bennett then quickly explained that he had been working with Chadwick's crew teams and the hard rowing had been good for toning his muscles.

Nigel, who was apparently uninterested in sports or in how Bennett's body was adapting to them, launched into another topic.

"Since we have four highly involved CU reps all gathered here together," he began in a formal tone, "maybe I can take the time to do a little informal research."

Though Salisa didn't voice it, she wanted to say, "Not here. Not today, Nigel! Why does everything have to be so businesslike with you?"

Good ol' Sophie, however, once again spoke what Salisa was too reserved to say. "Nigel, I don't want you to take this wrong, but I don't think any of us are in the mood to talk CU business right now. We're almost at the cathedral again," she said, looking around to get her bearings. "And then we can have our picnic. Don't you think that's a good idea, Salisa?"

"I don't know that I'd call Nigel's questions 'business,'" said Salisa, trying to soften the blow for Nigel, "but I do think that—"

"I agree with Salisa," Nigel interrupted. "This is the focal point of everyone's life here. I don't think it would hurt to take a few minutes to try to assess what's been happening in the CU groups we've been involved in." Nigel pulled a small notepad and a pen out of the blue bookbag he always carried with him and began asking Sophie questions.

Sophie, good sport that she was, obliged. Though it wasn't her topic of choice on this warm, sunny day, she did enjoy conversation, and at least Nigel was providing this for her.

With the two people she felt comfortable talking with engaged in their own conversation, Salisa rolled her jacket up into a small ball and laid her head down onto it. She hoped she was sending a signal of aloofness to Bennett. She watched the clouds drift by and felt the sun's rays sink into her skin. She'd almost forgotten what a warm sun felt like.

As if reading her mind, Bennett said, "Feels good, doesn't it, Salisa?"

She took her time propping herself up to look at him. "Yes," she said. He was staring at her intently. Sophie and Nigel had moved nearer to each other on one side of the punt, leaving Bennett directly in Salisa's line of view.

Though she didn't want to, she permitted herself the tiniest glance at Bennett's biceps and wished for a moment that she was Sophie and could follow her instincts more naturally. Bennett's long, tan arms pushed and pulled and steered and rested. As quickly as she could, Salisa shook herself out of her reverie. But it wasn't soon enough, a glance at Bennett told her—he'd been watching her.

"I've missed seeing you around," said Bennett softly. His tone was cordial, almost distant, but his eyes were pleading with Salisa to connect with him.

Instead, she looked over at Sophie and Nigel, who were starting to argue over the importance of numbers in Bible study groups. She looked a little more closely at Nigel. *Funny*, she thought, *I've always known that Nigel was thin, but compared to Bennett now, he looks almost sickly!* Nigel's thin, pale arms stuck out like sticks from his light blue, button-down dress shirt.

Salisa returned her attention to Bennett. He was still waiting for a reply to his statement, not pleading, just expecting acknowledgement.

"It's good to see you too, Bennett," Salisa replied evenly. "But to be honest," she said with a little more animation, "not seeing you keeps certain difficulties from cropping up."

Bennett, who was still using the pole to maneuver them around, looked at her gently. "You haven't even given me a chance to apologize for what happened."

Her radar for juicy information must have gone off, for Sophie suddenly turned toward Bennett and said, "Apologize for what?"

Before Salisa could even send Bennett a distress signal warning him not to betray their secret, Bennett said, "I think she's still mad because of the snowball fight we had in the Pennines."

And before Sophie could ask any questions, Nigel said, "Well, that's a pretty silly thing to hold a grudge about." Then he quickly turned back to finish a point he had been making with Sophie. Sophie looked undecided for a minute—each conversation was tempting her—and to Salisa's relief, she chose the one she was having with Nigel.

Salisa discreetly mouthed, "We'll talk later," and Bennett nodded.

"We're almost around the bend," Bennett called out, "so you two better be wrapping it up. No arguments during the picnic."

Salisa began unpacking their food and setting it out in the middle of the punt. As she did, she stole another glance at Bennett. He was facing the breeze he created by moving upstream and his eyes were almost closed. Salisa let herself look at his arms once more. A thought from somewhere deep inside her made her wonder what it would be like to be held by those strong, tan arms. She tried to push the image back down, but memories from the Pennines trip and some of their better times together started flooding her mind.

Then the stomach churn began. She had felt queasy a few times before, but the only time she could really remember was when she was feeling safe and cozy with Nigel at his house. But the force she was feeling now almost over- whelmed her. It was a feeling of attraction for Bennett, of wanting to be with him, to laugh with him, to talk with him, to play with him. Salisa tried to label the force, but the only word that came to mind was "passion." Passion! She had never figured this into any of her relationships, not even the five years she had spent with Dale.

As she was trying to define what was happening inside her, Bennett caught her gaze again. This time she let him see her blush. Salisa looked away. *I can only let him think what he will,* she resigned. She herself didn't know what she was thinking. How, then, could she control Bennett's thoughts?

She sighed audibly as she set the last bit of plastic silver- ware out. "Lunch is ready!" she called and, after a few quick interchanges between Nigel and Sophie, they came over. Bennett found a spot for the pole, and they all found places around the food and plates Salisa had neatly arranged.

"This looks great," said Bennett. Nigel, too, thanked Salisa and Sophie. "When we pray," said Bennett, "would any of you mind holding hands? I feel especially close to each of you right now. The year's ticking away, so I want to make the most of what little time we have left together." Nigel and Sophie nodded.

This was a somber thought, but each of the four moved in so they could grab hands. Now Salisa realized why Bennett had walked to the left of the boat—where Sophie had been sitting originally—instead of staying at the front of the boat, where he'd been punting. Taking a few extra seconds to "make sure the pole was secure," he had stayed long enough to cause Nigel and Sophie to take the places to the right and directly opposite Salisa.

Nigel assumed responsibility for the prayer and, as he prayed, Salisa felt one of Bennett's fingers lightly stroking her left hand. The proverbial spine-tingling chills that she had read about, but never experienced, gave her goosebumps even though her back was facing the sun. And as she looked around, certain that either Bennett was giving her funny looks or Sophie was taking notes for a later discussion, she was relieved to see that everyone's eyes were closed. So she followed suit.

The corned beef pasties were everything Sophie had promised they'd be—flaky and salty and better cold than anything similar cooked in America. The second course—strawberries smothered in Britain's thick, unsweetened cream—was a bit messier. Tiny, frosted cakes were the perfect dessert, washed down with paper cupfuls of Salisa's favorite, black currant juice.

Before long, a few of Bennett's better jokes had everyone in a giggly mood. At one point, they were laughing so hard that nobody noticed the punt pole roll off the boat. And nobody noticed that the punt itself was heading straight for a tangle of branches and trees.

## fourteen

"Look out!" Nigel was the first to call out since he was facing the impending catastrophe. But it was too late. The punt lurched as its left side ran aground, causing three of the passengers—and all of their food and jackets—to tumble off into the water. Fortunately, the river was only waist-deep where they were, so recovering was simply a matter of finding the ground and standing up.

Bennett had grabbed hold of his edge of the punt and had escaped falling in. As he tried to steady the boat and help the three back in, he suddenly fell back and started laughing.

Sophie and Nigel, who had been vying to be the first back on board, fell back in as their combined weight kept tipping the edge of the boat. Bennett was standing up, holding on to some of the overhanging tree branches for balance and trying to coach them between spasms of laughter.

"Only one at a time," he kept repeating. "I'll try to keep the weight balanced over here, but only one of you can get on at once."

Salisa, who didn't see the urgency in getting back on the boat once she was already wet, tried to gather what she could of their belongings. She had already thrown their soggy jackets into a heap in the corner of the punt. Not much else was salvageable.

Finally, Sophie and Nigel were on the boat and Bennett extended his hand to help Salisa up. She stood there in the waist-deep water, hands on her hips, looking up at him for a moment.

"What are you waiting for, Salisa?" cried Sophie. "You'll

catch cold if you stay in there."

"It's not that cold," said Bennett, who was looking at Salisa, trying to read her expression.

"Well, don't just stand there, Bennett," said Nigel. "Help her in."

"Yes," agreed Salisa, taking his hand. "What kind of gentleman are you—" And with that, she yanked on his hand. Bennett lost his balance and splashed into the river right next to Salisa. "To stand there high and dry while the rest of us are soaked!" she shouted as Bennett stood up to wipe the water from his face. Her face burst into a grin as she splashed Bennett with water to make sure he was as wet as the rest of them.

Instead of being mad, Bennett entered the water fight with the same gusto he had their snowball scuffle at the Pennines. After a few more splashing skirmishes, Bennett called a truce and began getting onto the punt. But Nigel and Sophie hadn't thought to move to the other side to balance the weight. Bennett weighed quite a bit more than any of the others so when Bennett tried to push himself up, he ended up dumping Nigel and Sophie back into the water.

Salisa thought the entire scene was hilarious. She was still standing in the water, totally drenched, thanks to Bennett, but she couldn't move because she was laughing so hard. Nigel and Sophie were once again trying to get on the boat, this time without Bennett's help. Once they had climbed up and properly positioned themselves in opposite corners, Bennett got on. Then he told Salisa she could help herself up since she had been the one to prolong what could have been a quick accident.

"No problem," said Salisa, as she pulled herself onto the punt. With three of them strategically placed on different corners of the punt, Salisa's weight didn't alter its stability. Once she was on, the four sat panting and Bennett tried to push the punt away from the shore so at least they could dry off in the sunlight.

"Where's the pole?" Salisa asked.

After a few minutes of looking, Bennett spotted it floating a short distance away. "We'll have to use our hands to paddle over there to get it," he said. "Or we can elect Salisa to swim over there." Despite being wet, Bennett still had a twinkle in his eye.

"Or we can push Bennett over and make him go get it," was Salisa's response and with that she lunged at him and the two went overboard again.

"Race ya' to the pole!" was Bennett's response as soon as they both had surfaced. There was no reply from Salisa except the taking of a deep breath of air and she was off. She doubted that she could beat Bennett—especially since he had been increasing his arm power with crew racing practice—but she gave it her best effort. The challenge had been too hard to resist. She swam with all her might toward the spot where she had seen the pole. The straining of her arm muscles and the deep gulps of air felt good, almost like a release from the tension she had been feeling ever since she knew she would have to be with Bennett again.

To her surprise, her hand touched the pole first. When she looked around, she saw Bennett right next to her.

"You let me win, didn't you?" she accused.

"I'll never tell," was his reply. There they were, face-to-face, with the sunlight glistening off their wet faces. Salisa felt another churn beginning and dangerous pictures start to form in her mind.

"Let's go back," said Salisa quickly. "I don't think Sophie and Nigel are enjoying this horseplay as much as we are." They both glanced over to the punt where Sophie and Nigel huddled, looking like dejected shipwreck victims.

Bennett continued to tread water, so Salisa started back toward the boat without him. Soon, he came alongside her, doing an odd sort of dog paddling since he was the one carrying the pole. They hoisted themselves up, found their respective corners, and, this time, stayed on the boat.

Had Sophie not been so afraid of fish, Salisa suspected that she would have joined her and Bennett in their water fight. As is was, however, she sided with Nigel, who said that if he couldn't enjoy the picnic dry, then he wouldn't enjoy it at all.

It was a long, quiet ride back to the docks.

"I think Nigel was totally shocked," Sophie told Salisa once they were back at St. Anne's, cleaning up.

"Soph, we were just having fun. I didn't go out there planning to ruin everyone's day."

"Well, on the bright side, I don't think you ruined Bennett's day. Are you sure there's nothing going on between you two?"

Salisa sat down on Sophie's bed and tried to dry her hair. She tried to sound nonchalant. "It's probably just a cultural thing, Soph. Somewhere along the line, maybe from American movies, Bennett and I were taught that water fights were fun. So that's all that was going on." As she crafted her explanation, Salisa had flashbacks of the times when she had thought Sophie and Bennett were the ones who were getting too silly. Somehow, it was much more fun being on this side of the accusation.

"I still think it was pretty inconsiderate of you." Sophie had her head upside down and was combing her hair, so Salisa couldn't see her expression.

"Acting up like that." A twinge of good-natured jealousy was present in Sophie's voice. "Even if you don't see it, I do. There's a definite spark building between you two."

Spark? Salisa didn't even think she knew what the word meant. "I think what you're seeing, Sophie, is two Americans who have a lot in common. We're both here for a year, both working through relationships at home, and. . .and that kind of thing."

"That doesn't sound like a very convincing argument to me," Sophie muttered, "considering you spent the first half of your time here telling me how much you *didn't* have in common."

Despite the desire to defend herself, Salisa let the subject of the water fight drop. She wanted to believe that what she was telling Sophie was the truth—that there really wasn't anything going on between Bennett and her—but if she were honest with herself, she wasn't so sure. True, she had never had so much fun as when she was battling Bennett in the elements, whether snow or water. But was fun grounds for a relationship? Salisa hardly thought so.

And Salisa had to remind herself that every time she gave in to frivolous flirting with Bennett, she was moving away from any real chances to develop a steady, stable relationship with someone like Nigel. She would have some patching up to do with him after the boat ride today, she surmised. But Nigel would understand. Salisa knew she could wriggle her way back into his good graces, with hardly more effort than when she had gone through the same kind of mishaps with Dale.

Later that night, as Salisa tossed and turned with the different scenes of men and friends floating through her mind, she finally gave up thinking and tried praying instead.

*God, you know the loose ends that I'm worried about right now. Please help me make intelligent choices concerning them.* Salisa paused, and then qualified her plea. *Okay, so maybe "intelligent" isn't the right adjective. People can make intelligent decisions that are wrong. . .I do that! So please help me make decisions that reflect Your will for my life. Help me get beyond fear and selfishness, staying in places that are safe, or running off to other places for the wrong reasons. Thanks in advance for Your guidance.*

When she felt herself falling asleep that night, Salisa had

the strangest feeling that she had "signed on the dotted line" somewhere, but she didn't know to whom or for what. She suspected that God knew, however, and she let that comforting thought pull her into sleep.

# fifteen

Salisa felt like a free bird. She was loaded on the train for London, after which she would make her way toward Dover, and then ferry across the English Channel to France. But Sophie was still yelling at her through the window.

"Be careful," mouthed Sophie. "You always seem to land right side up, just like a cat," she laughed. Sophie was pantomiming the words.

Salisa stood up and opened her window so they could talk more easily. "You can bet that I wouldn't miss my last few months here for anything," replied Salisa. "Between the end-of-the-year carnivals and all-night dances you've been telling me about. . .not to mention your play and the two weeks we have off while the students wait for their grades."

"It's *our* play," corrected Sophie. "And don't forget that we have the CU leaders' retreat sometime during those two weeks."

"How can I forget?" Salisa groaned. "Nigel has asked me to help out with some of the sessions. I have a few big books to read and notepads to fill during my long hours on the train."

Sophie looked curious. "That's strange. Last year Nigel worked with a local vicar for the retreat planning. I just assumed he would do so again."

"Why is it strange that I'm doing it then?"

"It just takes a lot of time," said Sophie. "You'll probably have to go up a day or two early with Nigel, that's all."

Now Salisa was intrigued as well. But her train was pulling out, so she stuck her hand out and gave Sophie one last wave.

"I'll see you soon, Soph," Salisa called out as the train began to pull away. "You've been the best."

"And you've kept the year interesting!"

"The best is yet to come," promised Salisa, but the chugging of the train drowned out her last few words. A few tears came to Salisa's eyes as Sophie became smaller and smaller and then finally disappeared from view.

Salisa settled into her seat. As she had done on her other train journeys, she leaned her head back and began to daydream about the places she was going to visit. This trip's destinations included Paris, Amsterdam, Munich, Salzburg, Vienna, Venice, Florence, Rome, and whatever cities in Germany she had time for in the end.

The train was making a few stops along its path to London, and at each one Salisa let her eyes flutter open when she heard the station's name announced over the train's intercom system. She liked to see who was getting off and on. But when the train stopped in Peterborough, she couldn't believe it—there was Bennett, wearing denims and a rugby shirt with horizontal stripes that made his chest look even bigger than usual.

Salisa slid down into her seat a little, hoping he hadn't seen her. What was he doing here? The only plausible reason Salisa could come up with was that maybe Bennett had left Abingdon a day or two early and had visited a friend somewhere in the area.

Regardless of why he was on her train, however, Salisa knew she wasn't in the mood to talk to him. This was supposed to be *her* trip, all by herself! Seeing Bennett this soon into it was not a good sign. A familiar mixture of dread and excitement began swirling in her stomach.

Salisa assumed that most of the seats in front of her were full since new passengers kept walking past her. Sure enough, Bennett came by too, and sat in the seat behind her.

She froze. He was bound to notice her at some point during the trip, and if she acted like she had already seen him, and chosen to ignore him, she would look foolish.

"Bennett!" she said, in the cheeriest voice she could muster. "What are you doing here?"

Bennett had been looking somewhat troubled, but as soon as he saw Salisa, his face broke into a smile. "Hey! I thought you had already left for Europe!"

Though Salisa was trying to guard herself against warming up to him too much, his smile, gentle and rich and soft, started to crumble her wall of resistance.

"I had to stay up until the very last day of the term to help Sophie finish up a few things for the play," said Salisa, "but you obviously escaped a little earlier."

"One of the guys on my floor—he's a new Christian—invited me to his house for a few days. Since he lives in Peterborough, which is right on the route to London, I just left with him on Tuesday and resumed the journey today. When I get to Victoria, I'll take a train out to the airport."

"So, you're heading back home?" queried Salisa.

The perplexed look returned to Bennett's face. "Yes," he said. "And I have to admit that I'm a little worried about it."

"The Hazel thing?"

"Yes."

"I'm planning to write my last letter to Dale, too," offered Salisa, using the opportunity to muster up her own resolve. "I figure that will give him some time before I come home . . .if I come home."

Bennett's face lit up. "You mean you're thinking about staying?"

Salisa quickly decided that if anyone could understand some of the choices she was facing right now, it was probably Bennett. So despite her reservations—she was getting used to pushing these aside—she lunged ahead.

"There's so much up in the air, Bennett. One of the other things I want to do on this trip is to beg God for some help on the decisions I'm facing. I don't know whether I should go back home to Pepperton, travel to somewhere exotic for another short-term mission assignment, or. . .I'm just trying to be open to anything."

"Are you really?" asked Bennett.

"Really what?"

"Open to anything?"

Salisa rolled her eyes. "Isn't that what I just said?"

"Give me an example."

Salisa started to protest but, after thinking about the question for a moment, she decided that answering it would be a good exercise for herself as well.

"For example," she began, "let's take Nigel. I like Nigel, I respect Nigel, and think he's a good Christian leader, but I've never been overwhelmed by him romantically. Not that I know for sure he's ever been romantically interested in me," Salisa quickly added. "But when we're alone, things happen." Salisa noticed Bennett's raised eyebrows and quickly clarified herself. "Nothing out of line, but he starts to open up. We've had some good talks in the CU office lately. I've talked with Maureen about this a little—she married a British man, you know—and she seems to think something is going on. She suspects that once the CU term is over, Nigel will find the necessary courage and propriety to tell me how he feels."

Bennett was listening intently.

Salisa took full advantage of his attention. "So I keep thinking to myself," she continued, "am I open to Nigel? And since I know Nigel is interested in missions, I ask myself, am I open to that? Those are the kinds of questions I think about."

"So you think that God's will is usually something that you don't think you want to do but maybe God will have you do it anyway."

Salisa didn't like the way Bennett had phrased it, but she said, "Well, kind of. . .sometimes." She paused to think. "It's just that we're sinful people, and we really can't be too sure about our own desires. That's how I think, anyway."

"Salisa," Bennett said gently, "I think you have it all wrong. Sometimes God works *through* our desires."

Salisa turned toward Bennett and wrinkled her nose. This was a new thought. She had always been so ordered in her thinking that this twist really jolted her. "I'll have to think about that," she said to Bennett. And then she picked up her journal to signal that she wanted to write.

Bennett acknowledged this. He began writing too, almost furiously on a scrap of paper he had pulled from his carry-on bag. Salisa was curious and wanted to ask him what he was writing, but she suspected that, knowing Bennett, this was just what he intended for her to do.

Both wrote until they heard "London, Victoria Station" announced over the speakers. Both then methodically put their pens and paper away and got ready to disembark.

"Well, this is it," said Salisa as the train began to pull slowly into the huge, multi-track Victoria station.

"Not yet, it isn't," said Bennett. He looked very nervous. Both stood up and met face-to-face in the center aisle. Before she could ask him what he meant by what he had just said, Bennett's one free hand came around the back of her head and pushed hers up toward his. This time his lips were much more expressive than they had been before. In fact, the emotion in Bennett's touch and kiss caused Salisa to almost stagger backward when he released her.

It couldn't have lasted more than a few seconds but, for Salisa, time had stopped. Nobody had ever kissed her this forcefully before—especially in public—and it was only by quickly turning her head to the right and left to assess reality that she was able to shake herself from what Bennett had just done.

Then an unexplained fury rose up within her. "Bennett, how could you do that?" she almost wailed, ignoring those around her. "After all I just told you?"

People began moving in front of them so Salisa followed, letting Bennett look at the back of her head.

"If you would think about what we just talked about, it makes perfect sense," said Bennett, lowly and quietly in her ear. When they had stepped off the train and walked away from the crowds hurrying to make a connecting train, Salisa turned to face Bennett.

"What makes sense is that you go home to Hazel and marry someone like you. Hazel manipulates you and when you're not around her, you try to manipulate other people. I don't know what you're trying to do by messing up our friendship like this," and at this point she looked like she was about ready to cry. Bennett went to hug her, but she pushed him away.

"I didn't want to be around other Americans on this trip," said Salisa, grasping at a sense of composure. "But when you and I found out that we could have fun together I thought, 'Okay, this won't be bad.' But twice you've done this now. And while we got over the first, I don't know that this will be repairable." Salisa was babbling and she knew it, but so many emotions were coming up to the surface that she only wanted to get them out once and for all.

"And another thing," said Salisa, her voice gaining strength and volume, "why do you always have to go running home on these breaks? Why don't you stay and experience some new cultures? Why do you always have to return to your well-to-do family, who can afford all these flights, and your perfect life with Hazel, who will be the perfect wife for you, instead of finding out who you really are?"

Salisa took a deep breath and resumed. "I did think,

really think at times, that you and I had a lot in common. But I'm glad I see now that we really don't. I would never play the kind of games you're playing with me. What are you trying to do?" her voice escalated with emotion. "Rack up another admirer so I can feel stupid when I see you back home? No thanks!"

With that, she turned and walked away, ignoring Bennett's "Salisa! You've got it all wrong! Let me try to explain."

Salisa couldn't remember being this distraught before. What had triggered it? That kiss! The memory of it filled her with all sorts of thoughts that she was simply not prepared to deal with right now. The schedule board said the connecting train to Dover was already in the station, so Salisa ran to it and climbed on, not looking back once to see if Bennett had followed her or was even watching her.

"What a rotten start to my trip," she mumbled to herself when she found a seat that was well away from other people. *Why did you let that happen, God*? she directed upward.

The thought then came to her that she had missed something. Missed what? What was there to miss? Bennett had kissed her, *really* kissed her this time, in public, without warning, without any consent on her part. Didn't she have a right to behave exactly as she had?

Something told her that she wasn't putting the puzzle pieces together right. But what was she doing wrong? She was calling things just as she saw them.

But maybe she wasn't seeing everything.

Salisa put her head back on her seat. She was just going to keep her eyes closed so she wouldn't have to see, or deal with, anything else. *It will work at least until I get to Dover*, she thought. And then, to her relief, she quickly fell asleep.

# sixteen

"Salisa! Over here." It was Sophie, waving from almost the exact place where she had waved Salisa off, five weeks before. Sophie ran up to her American friend.

"My goodness!" she held Salisa at arm's length. "Are you thin and brown! What'd you do? Sit in Italy the whole time and forget to eat?"

"Here," said Salisa, handing Sophie a bag full of books. "Carrying these all over Europe proved to be a mistake. I think I have biceps as big as a man's now. But I got a lot of work done. I think I have some really good ideas for the CU retreat."

"No talk about work until I hear about all your adventures," Sophie said firmly. Sophie and Salisa passed through the people waiting for cabs and began to walk down the hill toward town. "Go ahead," prompted Sophie, "start from the beginning."

"Oh, Soph," Salisa almost moaned. "I don't know where to start. It's good, no, great to be back in Abingdon, but I had the most magical time." For a brief moment, Salisa thought about starting at the real beginning of her trip, when she had run into Bennett on the train, but she decided against it. She had done quite a bit of soul-searching during the Easter holidays, and she was not about to dredge up any unpleasant memories and the emotions they brought with them.

"What was nice about this trip was that I was finally alone," began Salisa. "Nobody was around to confuse me." She paused. "And I wrote Dale the final letter."

"You did?"

Salisa looked at Sophie and smiled with peace and confidence. "It was the right thing to do. I'm sure of it. Even if I return home now, I'll—"

"If?" Sophie jumped on the word. "You mean you might stay?"

Salisa bit her lip. "Now you can't get all excited, Soph. I'm just trying to be open. If I'm meant to go home, I'll go home. But somehow I feel like I might end up somewhere else."

"Like where?" Sophie's bright eyes showed no sign of tiredness, even though she was carrying two of Salisa's three bags.

"I don't know, Soph. We'll see what turns up. I understand that a bunch of short-term requests come through the CU office every spring. I'll start by looking through those."

"Come to Bangladesh with me, Salisa!" Sophie almost yelled, grabbing Salisa's arm.

"You're going for sure then?"

"It's almost for sure. There's a girls' school in Dhaka that needs an English and Bible teacher, so it looks like that's going to work out. I bet they could use someone like you too, Salisa. Why don't you inquire?"

"I'll look into it, Soph."

They had reached the edge of town. They descended the cement steps under the Gates Street Bridge in order to connect with the footpath that led up to St. Anne's. Salisa and Sophie walked in silence for a few minutes, simply soaking up the moist smell of the banks and the sight of the riverbank's trees, now green and fluffy with leaves.

"So tell me about your trip," Sophie tried again. "You know once we're at St. Anne's we're going to be busy with all our end-of-the-year projects."

Salisa looked ahead of her. They were about fifteen minutes from St. Anne's. "Okay," she said. "I don't want to talk about it too much because that will spoil the solitude of it.

But here's the condensed version."

Salisa told Sophie about Paris and Lucerne, and Venice and Florence, and finally Rome, where she had stayed the longest.

"It was marvelous, Soph," Salisa said. "I had a small, cozy room with a balcony, and I spent a lot of early mornings and early evenings out there, just writing and reading and thinking. It was just me and God, and I think I finally sat still long enough to listen to Him."

"And what did He say?"

"That I just need to be open to what He has planned. That's why I'm open to seeing what other short-term missionary needs come up. No plans, no promises."

"Well, there's not a lot of time left," reminded Sophie. "There's about six weeks of classes during which, may I remind you, we have to wrap up the play, and then there are exams, then ball season, then the end. Hurray!"

"Tell me more about these 'balls,' Sophie. The only ball Americans get to hear about is the one in the Cinderella story. I can't believe there are places that still have traditions like that." Salisa could tell that Sophie was torn between wanting to hear more about Salisa's trip to Europe and prattling on about the balls. "I've told you the highlights of my trip, Soph," Salisa encouraged. "There's not much more to tell that's exciting."

"Okay," agreed Sophie. She took a deep breath. "Each college has their own ball and they range in quality."

"How so?"

"Well, Castle College, since it has the most exotic setting and the highest number of well-to-do students, has the best. They have a big band, a full breakfast after the all-night ball dance, and a Scottish piper who plays up on the castle wall while everyone eats a delicious Scottish breakfast.

"St. Anne's is okay. Since it is one of the older colleges, it has a lot of charm and a lot of men consider it a privilege to get invited to the garden party we host the day after the ball. You'll see a lot of schmoozing going on around here now that it's the last term."

"Schmoozing?"

"People start hinting that they'd like to go to each other's balls. Each one has something to offer. Chadwick, for example, almost always has a carnival on its grounds."

"Really?"

"And most have some sort of all-night entertainment and games going on. It's really the best time of the year."

"I can imagine," mused Salisa. "Everyone goes to one of the balls then?"

"Not everyone," she admitted. "It can get expensive, with a ball gown and all." She paused, but then continued as if she had already given the matter some thought. "If I don't get invited by someone special, I might not go. But then again," she looked up to Salisa cheerily, "a lot of people go in mixed groups. That's kind of nice. It takes some of the pressure off of trying to have this wonderfully romantic evening."

Since writing Dale, Salisa had found herself vaguely dreaming for a relationship that would work out. "But a wonderfully romantic evening would be fun now and then," she joked. And Sophie agreed. But Sophie gave her friend a funny look out of the corner of her eye.

"I know what you're going to say, Soph," Salisa muttered. "But don't say it. I think I sat out in that wonderful Italian sun just a little too long."

But Sophie just gave her a hug. "I knew you had it in you," was all she said.


"Salisa, why don't we leave early enough to take a hike around one of the lakes," Nigel suggested one day as they were collating the last of the handouts they planned to take along on the CU retreat. "Since you haven't been to the

Lake District yet, I want to make sure you have plenty of time for at least one good hike."

As Salisa had tried to explain to Bennett on the train, she was experiencing increasingly warm feelings toward Nigel. Maybe it was the way he threw himself into his CU position or his steadfast outlook on life. Or maybe it was his eagerness to include Salisa in his CU plans which, in this case, was resulting in her getting to spend extra time in a part of England she hadn't visited yet.

"Going early sounds like a great idea, Nigel," she told him. "What time are we talking then? Thursday morning?"

"I was thinking more like Wednesday."

"Wednesday?"

"The sooner, the better," said Nigel. "Salisa, you've got to see it. Once you do, you'll wish you had gone up a week early."

Nigel was right. She and Nigel arrived midafternoon that Wednesday, just in time to take a short walk before dinner. They explored the area around the guest house where the group would be staying.

Salisa had seen pictures of the Lake District, but being there in person locked the scene in her senses forever. It was a typical lake-in-the-hills setting, but the ancient stone fences, the peculiar damp yet sunny weather, and the scattered-about stone cottages all made it seem as if it were a page out of *Hansel and Gretel*. William Wordsworth's favorite hideaway was near a small town called Grasmere, and once Salisa had been there, it was easy to see what had inspired his image-rich poetry.

"Nigel," Salisa breathed on their first real hike off the guest house property. The space and the scalloped hills overwhelmed her. She was attempting to inhale everything all at once when a breeze floated over the nearby lake, introducing Salisa to a number of new, intermingled meadow-like scents. She couldn't distinguish, or know, what was what, but she wanted to remember it forever. And she told Nigel so.

"Salisa," he said, lightly touching her hand. "This seems to be as good a time as any to tell you something," he began. "How would you like to be able to come back here frequently. . .even often?"

She gave Nigel a questioning look, wanting him to explain and yet starting to fear that it might be something she didn't want to hear.

"I would just like to know if I could see you more after this year is over, that's all," said Nigel.

Salisa breathed a sigh of relief. That was all! Nigel simply wanted to maintain the friendship. "Sure, Nigel," she responded, smiling again. It was as if the sun returned from a brief duck into the clouds. She took his arm and they began walking down a small, sandy path that seemed to lead around the lake.

"In fact," she continued several minutes after she had last spoken, "I haven't told you this yet, but I'm thinking about staying around for another year. Somewhere. I'm not sure where, but I think God may be telling me to be ready to go . . .or stay here."

Nigel turned to stare at Salisa while they continued walking.

"What's wrong?" she asked.

Nigel turned to her with a boyish smile. "Salisa," he said, "why don't you come with me to India? My term there is all set. I'll be working with some students there and—"

"Funny you should say that," Salisa interrupted. "Sophie wanted me to go with her to Bangladesh. Will you and she plan to see each other? You won't be that far apart." She continued to walk down the trail noticing the different kinds of wildflowers that bordered the worn path.

When Nigel didn't answer right away, Salisa turned toward him to figure out why. He was intently watching the ground. His expression was tight, almost contorted.

Sensing her stare, Nigel turned nervously to meet it. "But I wasn't thinking of the three of us getting together," he stammered. "I was thinking of. . .you and me."

"The two of us?"

Nigel nodded.

"As in *together*?"

Nigel nodded again. "As in *really* together," he added.

"As in *married*?" Salisa almost screamed. "Nigel, are you proposing to me?"

Once more, the head bobbed up and down.

"I can't believe it," Salisa muttered. Here she had just extricated herself from one proposal only to land right in the middle of another one. What next?

The thought flashed through her mind that she needed to be open. She could hear her own words echoing around her: "I'm not sure what it is God wants me to do, but I'm going to try to be open about it."

Could God be asking her to consider marrying Nigel? It didn't make sense. It seemed too much like. . .how it had been with Dale.

But maybe that hadn't been all bad. Confortable, predictable, and dependable relationships certainly had their benefits. Maybe all God was trying to teach her was not to tie herself down to the security of Pepperton.

"Salisa?" Nigel was looking at here, eyes wide with wonder, hope. "You didn't say no, right?"

Slowly, Salisa shook her head back and forth. "No, I didn't say no." *Not yet anyway*, she added in her mind.

"Good!" said Nigel, throwing his arms around her. Salisa felt like she was suffocating, but she didn't say anything.

"I'm. . .I'm just so happy!" he was repeating over and over again.

"Nigel," she said, pushing him away from her. "I need some time to think about this. It's so sudden. You have to give me. . .and God. . .some time to come up with the right answer."

Nigel looked as if he had already received his answer. He was beaming and still holding one of Salisa's hands.

"Salisa," he said, following her name with a deep breath. "You can take all the time you need to feel good about this decision. I'll wait for you. Even if you decide to go somewhere else for a year. . .that's okay. I've spent a year thinking about this and another year's wait wouldn't be any trouble at all." He started laughing to himself. "Why, look at Jacob! He worked fourteen years for the wife he wanted! What's two?"

*This is serious,* thought Salisa. *Oh well, Lord,* she prayed silently as they continued to walk, *as long as I don't get myself into something too quickly. This year's revealed a lot. Who knows what changes another year would bring?*

With great effort, Salisa dismissed from her mind the seriousness of Nigel's affections for her and concentrated instead on enjoying every blissful detail of the Lake District. She had a strange sense of peace that the issue with Nigel would resolve itself soon.

The retreat went well, mostly because Salisa and Nigel made a good planning team. Nigel did most of the speaking with Salisa adding creative touches such as impromptu plays, silly songs, or slide shows when appropriate. The election of new officers went smoothly, too, and Nigel later apologized for proposing before their CU terms were officially over.

"Now I can tell people about it!" he exclaimed after he had apologized.

Salisa froze. "Not so fast, Nigel," she warned. "You told me you would give me some time on this. What's the use of telling everyone about it now if it could be years away?"

Though Nigel had seemed to think two years was "nothing" only a few days ago, he was sobered. "You're right, I guess." But he did ask Salisa if he could confide in one person, a prayer partner. Salisa supposed that was okay.

The rest of the weekend passed smoothly. The large turnout—about seventy-five undergraduate and graduate representatives along with various faculty sponsors—kept Salisa from accidentally bumping into Bennett, and her leadership jobs gave her the perfect excuse to stay behind the scenes rather than mingle. But Bennett, with his uncanny timing, tapped her on the shoulder just as she was putting her luggage into the university car she and Nigel had driven to the retreat.

"Hi, Sal," he said.

She turned to face him. Up close, Salisa could see the tan on his face, and the tee shirt he had on gave his well-figured arms unusual prominence. For an instant, Salisa remembered their kiss on the train. . .and the feelings of Bennett's arms as they pulled her toward him.

"I just wanted to tell you that I think you and Nigel did a great job," said Bennett. He was somewhat cool but the warmth behind his eyes and smile seeped through. "We didn't have a chance to talk much during these three days, so. . . ." He ended his unfinished sentence with a smile and a shrug.

Salisa relieved the awkward moment. "Thanks, Bennett," she said, turning to the packing she had started. "I'm glad you enjoyed it. Nigel and I had a good time planning it."

"That's what Nigel said," Bennett offered to her back side. "And he also mentioned that the two of you are considering, umm. . .some commitments."

Salisa turned to face him and her eyes narrowed. Since when had Nigel and Bennett become prayer partners? She couldn't decide who she was mad at more, Nigel or Bennett. But since Bennett was the one standing in front of her, he got the brunt of her disgruntledness.

"And what if we are?" she said. "I haven't made any final decisions yet, and I'd appreciate it if both you and he would quit talking about it until I do!"

"Good for you, Sal—I mean, I think that's wise that you're taking some time to think about it. Time can make a lot of things clear."

Salisa studied him for a minute. It was a shame that somebody so hard to get along with was trapped in such a good-looking package.

"Bennett," she said evenly, "I appreciate your concern, but I hardly think you're an expert on romance." She paused for effect. "For example, I don't know if you remember or not, but a long time ago, you and I talked about the decisions we had to make regarding people back home. I've done what I set out to do, but something tells me you're still hanging on to Hazel." Salisa meant for her tone to accuse, and it did.

"She's the one hanging on," said Bennett. There was a tinge of sadness in his eyes. "It was tough at Easter. Maybe Nigel told you about it?"

Salisa was rubbing her hands where the rough handle on her suitcase had cut into them. "Believe it or not, Bennett, we don't spend all our time talking about you. We have enough of our own dilemmas to work on."

Bennett unintentionally let one of his million-dollar smiles slip out before looking down and kicking an imaginary soccer ball.

"Well, I congratulate you on making a firm decision about Dale. I did my best to be as brave, Salisa," he said. "Hazel still says she wants a ring when our term ends here in June ,and I made it clear I wasn't thinking along the same lines."

"So what are you going to do?" Salisa tried to sound disinterested.

"Go ahead with my plans," replied Bennett. "I can't make her accept the truth. Until she sees me actually doing them, she won't face the truth. I wish it weren't this way, but she's the one making it hard for herself."

"Hmm," acknowledged Salisa. "That's tough." She looked around. Others were starting to pull away amid waves and cheers of "See you back at the university."

Bennett caught the cue and excused himself. "Like I said, great job, Salisa," he repeated, trying to end the conversation on a casual note.

"Thanks," was all Salisa offered in return.

When she and Nigel were settled into the car for the five-hour drive back to Abingdon, it wasn't long before Nigel reached over and took her hand. Seeing the situation as a barometer for her own feelings, Salisa let him hold it. She analyzed her reactions—or lack of them—and tried talking to God about the matter.

But something didn't seem right. Something was missing.

She tried releasing her hand and softly touching Nigel's hair while she talked to him. Still, nothing. *Maybe it's just because we're so comfortable with each other*, Salisa rationalized. *Or because he's known as a spiritual leader around Abingdon. Or. . .because I don't care about him the way I need to.*

Could she ever?

She had no idea. God would have to make things crystal clear *soon* or she was going to leave Abingdon more mixed up than when she came.

# seventeen

Ball preparations were in full swing when the CU leaders returned from their retreat. Watching people run around was enough to take Salisa's mind off all her worries—even Nigel. Exams were over, and students were buying their ball garb and making plans in earnest. Nigel had been hinting that it would be nice if they could go to Chadwick's ball together, exclusively, but Salisa had wriggled out of it by saying that it would be one of the last times she had to be with her friends. Salisa had then quickly enlisted Sophie to pull together such a group, which Sophie gladly did.

Sophie was well prepared for the play, but Salisa couldn't tear her away from the set. So she left Sophie to putter about with meaningless details while she finished up some end-of-the-year records in her tutorial office. She was just getting ready to clean off her desk for the last time and lock up, when she heard a soft knock on the door.

"Come in," she said tentatively. She looked around her for the desk copy of her weekly sign-up sheet. No one had been in for the last few days so Salisa had figured that everyone's post-examination work had been completed.

A thin, sandy-haired young man came in. "Hello," Salisa said brightly. "Can I help you?"

"Are you Salisa Vrenden?" he asked.

"Yes, that's me."

Immediately the young man pulled up a chair and sat down to face Salisa across her desk. He looked forlorn yet ornery ,and Salisa couldn't figure out how the two fit together.

"You've got to help me," he said in a posh accent that Salisa had picked up among some of the more affluent students. "I'm trying to finish up this essay for my first-year drama class and it's just not working! And I have to turn it in today!"

"Calm down, calm down," Salisa almost laughed. "You'll have to give me a little more information if you expect me to try to help you. Now, who's this for?"

The boy thought for a moment. "Umm, Dr. Crane."

"And what is it he wants you to do? I'm pretty familiar with the assignments he gave this year. We should be able to work something out."

"It's like this." He cleared his throat. "We're supposed to take one of the Shakespeare plays we studied this year and write a modern rendition of it. The trick is to pick out all the great themes and show that we understand them and can translate them into situations that happen today."

Salisa shook her head. She couldn't recall ever working on an assignment like this for one of Dr. Crane's students.

"Can you run that by me one more time?" Salisa asked. She tried to listen hard and it seemed like the more the student talked, the more she realized that he already had a firm idea in mind.

"So, you'd like to write about a modern hero that wins over the heroine in a way that reveals that *he's* the only one who truly knows her."

"Right!" The student slumped in his chair in relief.

"It seems to me that you know the kind of themes you have a handle on," Salisa continued to diagnose, "so it's really a matter of finding a play that fits what you can do. That's really a backward way of going about it and not very orthodox, I'm sure, but at this late date, it might work."

The student grinned and nodded.

"So, did you have any plays in mind. . .any that you really liked?" asked Salisa. "Maybe we can start by taking a look at those."

The student gave Salisa a blank look. When he saw her

growing agitated, he offered, "*Romeo and Juliet?*"

Now it was Salisa's turn to sit back in her chair. It was clear that this student intended to skate by with only the minimum of effort. But, just then, a breeze from her window that overlooked the river floated past her and the calming scent of mud and wet grasses gave her a sliver of compassion for the young man.

"Okay," she said. "Let me think for a moment." But it took only a few seconds for her mind to begin to drift toward Sophie's play, *A Midsummer Night's Dream*, which was to be performed that evening.

"I have some ideas," she said after making a few notes on a piece of paper. "But they certainly aren't great literary overtures. Take them for what they're worth and try to come up with something your professor will like. I wasn't hired to do this sort of thing, but I'll do my best." Salisa then proceeded to outline the plot of *A Midsummer Night's Dream*, and showed how the romantic mix-ups between four of the primary characters—the men Lysander and Demetrius and the women Hermia and Helena—could have been prevented.

"They were all relying on the *appearances* of love that the fairies' magic potion caused," explained Salisa. "It's quite comic. All the characters become tangled up in the wrong romances." She tried to draw a chart that showed how tangled the relationships became in the course of just a few acts.

"But in your modern play, you could figure out a way for the hero to be the one to really discover what it is that makes his heroine completely different from anybody else." Salisa stopped to think. "He has to uncover good secrets about her. . .maybe even secrets that she isn't aware of . . .then expose them at just the right moment, proclaiming his love. How's that?" Salisa gave her student a triumphant look.

Her student was frantically scribbling down notes. When he looked up, he said, "But I need some more specifics. Such as what *kinds* of secrets?"

"But then I'll be doing all the work for you!" Salisa exclaimed good naturedly. "Why don't you take the ideas I've given you, try to write a draft, and if you still need more help, I can plan to be here around this time tomorrow." She looked at her watch and made another note on a sheet of paper. She would be back tomorrow afternoon anyway to help Sophie tear down the set. "If you're still having trouble, check back with me then. But if you're not here by three, I'll be gone. It's the big Ball Night, you know!"

"But I'm almost positive that I am going to need more help on my paper," the student stammered.

"I hope you have more faith in yourself than that," Salisa chuckled, waving him out the door. "I'm not going to help you any more until you've at least given it a try. But come find me if you absolutely have to."

Salisa spent part of the following day comforting Sophie who kept going over and over the few mistakes her performers had made and what could have prevented them. At three o'clock, after finally teasing Sophie out of her mood and convincing her of the play's obvious success, Salisa slipped away to see if the student she had met with yesterday had returned. He had, and was waiting outside her office door.

"It's the same dilemma I told you about yesterday," he complained, as Salisa unlocked the door and motioned for him to take a seat. "I simply need help with a few more specifics. I can't think like a woman! What will win the heroine over?"

Salisa had to laugh at his enthusiasm. Never had she seen a student take such a personal interest in a paper.

"I need some really creative ideas," the student

continued, settling into his chair with a notepad and pencil. "Like. . .what would work for you, Miss Vrenden?"

After a few more minutes of persistent questions, Salisa finally allowed herself to drift into her imagination. Since *A Midsummer Night's Dream* was still foremost in her mind, some of her ideas ran parallel to symbols in the play.

"How about having the hero steal his heroine away to someplace like the Botanical Gardens?" Salisa suggested. Abingdon's Botanical Gardens were a short walk away from St. Anne's and a favorite haunt of students. "Gardens are sort of like the romantic fairy woods from *A Midsummer Night's Dream*." Her guest prodded her on, pleading for "more specifics."

"He could read her some poetry, or something like that," Salisa offered. "That's always charming." The student scribbled this down. She eventually supplied what he needed, for he abruptly got up to leave when she had listed idea number four.

"Thanks, Miss Vrenden," he said as he left. "I better get started working on this. In the meantime, I hope all your dreams come true."

*What a strange student,* Salisa thought as he closed the door behind him. He had certainly been an interesting end to her tutoring career. Rushing, but still watching for accuracy in spelling and scores, Salisa quickly finished the few records she hadn't finished the day before. She put her files in the academic dean's office and locked her office door for the last time.

"At least I have a few more times in you," she said aloud, poking her head into the open doorway of the CU office as she passed by.

"Oh, hi, Bennett." Salisa was startled. She hadn't expected to see anyone in the office on such a beautiful day. Bennett said hi back, but he looked so engrossed in what he was working on that Salisa didn't stop to talk. *Just as well,* she thought, although something in her almost pulled her back.

Had her plastic sandals not been clicking so loudly down the steps outside the office, Salisa would have been sure she heard voices back in the office. But she had only seen Bennett there. She stopped, and so did the voices she thought she had heard.

*Time's a wastin,'* she reminded herself. It was time to turn her imagination off. It was ball tonight and, romance or not, she was going to enjoy every last minute of it.

# eighteen

"Does my hair look okay when I put the scarf on this way, Soph?" Salisa was kneeling so Sophie could get a better look at the back of her head.

"It looks absolutely brilliant," replied Sophie. "Your hair's really gotten long this year. The french braid in the back with swoops in the front looks perfectly elegant."

Salisa looked over to the mirror on the back of Sophie's door. The satin, knee-length dress hugged her trim body, but the tucks and pleats were filled out in all the right places. The deep redness of it—almost a burgundy—brought out the blond highlights in her hair yet added interest to her eyes, making them appear darker and larger.

"Why don't you dress up more often?" Sophie asked.

"Like this?"

"No, just with bright colors and tucks and pleats. . .that kind of thing," Sophie explained. "All the men will be saying, 'Now, who's this?' They won't recognize that it's the CU rep from St. Anne's who practically lived in her Levis and Michigan sweatshirt all year."

"And ponytail," added Salisa. Then she walked over to the bed where Sophie was nervously trying to paint her nails. "How do you get yours so smooth?" she wailed.

"Here, let me help. I'm practically ready."

When Sophie left to go dry her nails by the bathroom's heater, Salisa sat back on the almost empty bed and surveyed the room. Clothes were strewn everywhere and shoes and nylons and jewelry had been gone through in search of *the* perfect accessories. Getting ready for their first ball had been everything Salisa had hoped it would be—giggles, expectations, and excessive self-indulgence. The only miss-ing ingredient had been the romantic angle that both had agreed they were probably better off without.

Sophie came running in. "I heard Bennett and Nigel down-stairs," she said breathlessly. "I think there are some other people with them. Are we ready? Here, shove some of this under the bed." Sophie went around frantically trying to hide some of the evidence of their poor decision-making skills.

Salisa hadn't wanted to be with Bennett for Ball Night, but rather than make a scene when Sophie proposed includ-ing him, she had just made sure they were with a big enough group. A few other students in St. Anne's knew men in Chadwick, so a group of a dozen or so had agreed to attend together.

Sophie jumped when the knock on the door came.

"Relax," Salisa whispered. "You knew they were com-ing. Now just be calm and enjoy yourself." Salisa opened the door and found herself standing face-to-face with Bennett. In a dark blue suit, he looked taller than usual. The cut of his jacket accentuated his shoulders and his tan face was smooth and warm in contrast to his crisp, white shirt. Though he was worth staring at, Salisa didn't want Bennett to know this.

"Come in," she said graciously. "I don't believe I've ever seen you in a suit before, Bennett."

Sophie finished what Salisa was thinking but didn't say. "You look great!"

Salisa was watching Nigel and the few other men from Chadwick trail in, so she hadn't been watching Bennett's reaction as he looked at her and Sophie to assess their efforts. "Hi, Nigel," Salisa was saying. "And this is? Hi, Marty. And John. This is going to be fun. Sophie? Are you ready to go?" When Salisa went to pick up her purse from the bed, she had to say "excuse me" to Bennett, who had chosen to stand in the few cleared-away feet of space in front of Sophie's bed. He moved, just enough to let her get what she needed. The others were chattering, so no one heard him whisper, "You look great, Salisa. It's going to be hard to keep from staring at you all night!"

"Well, you're going to have to," Salisa said audibly. She was trying desperately to deter him. But he wasn't embarrassed. "Salisa, you're so silly," was all he said.

Salisa purposely walked with Nigel as they left St. Anne's, asking him how his day had been. His suit was a little too big on him, and Salisa could tell that the extravagance of the evening was making him nervous.

"Let's not stay out too late tonight, Salisa," he said. "These parties tend to get kind of wild as the night goes on."

Salisa was disappointed by his lack of enthusiasm. "We'll see," was all she said. "You might have more fun than you think."

"It will be fun because I'm with you," Nigel said, giving her a timid smile as they got into the taxi that was waiting for them outside. Salisa watched as Bennett and Sophie got into the back seat of the second one. They were both already laughing. Sophie had admitted that she wanted to be with Bennett as much as possible; she had always found him attractive and had heard rumors that he was good at ballroom dancing. Salisa felt a twinge of restlessness well up inside her, but she quickly dismissed it as excitement about the evening.

"Do you like my new dress, Nigel?" She turned and gave him a bright smile. "Sophie and I went shopping together. We've had so much fun getting ready for this."

"It's. . .it's kind of racy," Nigel said, giving her a look that was almost disapproving.

Salisa's eyes widened with defense and amazement. "It's a foot longer than most of the dresses I've seen around here and you certainly can't say that it's tight!" As she looked at

Nigel, she could tell that he was getting ready to say something else about the makeup on her eyes. She looked away.

"It's just not my style, Salisa," Nigel continued, not realizing that he was putting a damper on Salisa's spirit. "Don't
take it personally."

Salisa looked back at Nigel, trying to convince herself
that any man who would wear white socks with a cornflower blue suit and a tie with fishes on it that didn't go
with anything else didn't know what style was anyway. But
then she remembered Nigel's spiritual wisdom and wondered if she was simply being too "worldly."

Bennett and Sophie were already waiting for them at
Chadwick; they must have found one of Abingdon's more
rambunctious cabbies. Salisa could hear the tinkling of carnival music the minute her car door was opened.

"Welcome to Chadwick's magical ball," Bennett was saying as he helped Salisa out of the back seat of the cab. Then
in a grand tone he said, "I'm going to make sure everyone
has the time of their lives." After sweeping his arm to indicate the wonders behind him, his eyes crinkled up as he
laughed. "I was on the planning committee," he said meekly.
"So I guess I'm a little biased. But I *do* happen to know
where all the secret corners are. . .and all the best tables to
sit at for the hors d'oeuvres and desserts."

"You mean we're not having one big meal, like usual?"
Nigel asked.

"That's something new that we're trying," said Bennett
proudly. "It's a nine-course meal spread out throughout the
entire evening. You have to stay up the whole night to get
dessert!"

Nigel look dismayed. "I probably won't stay the whole
time," he admitted to Salisa, obviously waiting for her to
agree to leave with him.

"Well, I intend to be up until dawn," said Salisa with zest.
She hadn't promised to be Nigel's "date." She looked over

at Sophie, who was nodding and smiling. If nothing else, Salisa would stick with Sophie. They'd take a cab back to St. Anne's by themselves if they had to.

The group began to walk under the college's gateway, which had been decorated with streamers and balloons. Everywhere they looked, they could see merry-go-rounds, food booths, and pretty benches in front of flowering bushes where couples or groups could have their pictures taken. The college grounds, which sloped from an asphalt road of quaint classrooms and offices down toward the river, were already a mass of moving colorful bodies.

Salisa thought she had encountered, and mastered, most of England's favorite ethnic foods, but new varieties of cakes and pastries, savory appetizers, and luscious fruit ices met her at every corner. The entertainers, from small string ensembles to drama sketches, captured her attention, and even Nigel seemed to be having a good time. But after the fireworks went off at midnight, he quickly turned into a pumpkin. He tried his best to get Salisa to call it a night, too, but to no avail.

"I'm staying, and that's it!" she finally said firmly. "Sophie and I are determined to make it until sunrise. Right, Soph?"

But when she turned to get Sophie's agreement, Salisa couldn't find her. Most of the group she had been with was in line for their fifth ride on the Ferris wheel, but she didn't see Sophie. Oh, well. She was probably taking in a few rides with some of her friends from the other colleges.

"Really, Nigel, I'll be fine. I'll catch up with you sometime tomorrow. You go on up."

"It's just that I'm so tired," he almost moaned. He rubbed his eyes.

"I know you are. I could tell that from the minute you walked into Sophie's room. Now, get up there and get a good night's sleep. And don't feel bad! Knowing you, you have plenty of things to do tomorrow."

Nigel gave her a wan look. "You don't think I'm a bad ball partner?"

"No, not at all," Salisa said. And then she pushed him away. "Now, go on, scoot! We'll talk tomorrow." Then she turned to grab a place in line with the others from St. Anne's and Chadwick.

She couldn't have been there more than a minute when she felt a large hand grab her own. A familiar voice said, "I thought he'd never leave. Come on." It was Bennett, and Salisa let him pull her from the line and away toward a group of trees that lined the river at the edge of Chadwick's campus.

"Bennett! Wait! What are we doing?" Salisa tried to stiffen as she remembered how much she sometimes disliked Bennett but the abandonment with which he was pulling her away appealed to her.

Bennett had only looked back and smiled in response to her last question, so she tried again. "Where are you taking me?" Just then, they reached the stony path that ran along the river's edge, down past some of the college boathouses, through town, and up toward Mill Bend Bridge. Bennett stopped to look at her. It was dark, but the light from the almost-full moon illuminated his face. "Where do you think I'm taking you, my lady in red?"

Salisa took a deep breath. "I know where I would like to go," she answered. Her voice was low with restrained excitement.

"So do I," said Bennett. And he offered his arm for her to take.

# nineteen

Salisa was thrilled at being on the footpath in the middle of
the night. Many times she had begged Sophie to go with her
on a late-night walk along the river, but every time Sophie
had refused. She said it was too dangerous. Now that she
had a male escort, and a fairly large one at that, Salisa wanted
to wander the entire footpath, as far as it would take her!
Her desire to be by the river in the middle of the night out-
weighed her desire to send Bennett away.

*Just for a few minutes*, Salisa argued with her more
rational side. *Then I'll ask him to turn back soon and thank
him for the pleasant evening walk.*

Bennett didn't interrupt her enjoyment of the silence and
the dark. Salisa's "few minutes" quickly turned into twenty.
Soon, Salisa saw Mill Bend Bridge in the distance. She let
herself smile with anticipation.

"Are you happy, Salisa?" he asked gently.

"I'm not going to *not* smile just because I'm trying to
prove something to you, Bennett Havana."

"What are you trying to prove to me, Salisa?" Bennett asked.
"Aren't you really trying to prove something to yourself?"

"Bennett, please don't try to make me defensive again."
Suddenly Salisa decided that she didn't like the feeling of
Bennett holding her hand. She took it away. Bennett didn't
react; he just let her do or say whatever she wanted. "You're
always trying to talk me into things I'm not sure about."

Bennett was silent until Salisa could stand it no longer.
"Why aren't you disagreeing with me?" she asked.

"Because I don't want to, Salisa. You already think I'm
antagonistic. And I don't know how to correct that

impression. So I'll just try to be quiet. I only want you to enjoy this evening. That's all I want."

For a moment Salisa thought about how different Nigel and Bennett were from each other. Every desire she had had for the evening seemed to be at odds from what Nigel was planning. And here was Bennett, somehow knowing what she wanted to do, and enabling her to do it. Then something clicked.

"Bennett, why do you think Nigel was so tired this evening? I know he's not a night owl, but this is a big night. Midnight is too early to leave a ball."

"I thought you'd ask sooner or later," said Bennett. "And though you'll call me manipulative, I'll confess that I kept him up lately, playing pinochle."

"On purpose?"

"What do you think, Salisa?" He was smiling calmly, not trying to prove anything, it seemed. Then he looked ahead, tossed his head back, and took a deep breath of the cool air.

"I don't understand you, Bennett," Salisa said.

"Don't try," he responded. "Just enjoy the evening." Then he took her hand again and Salisa didn't pull away. He led her up to Mill Bend Bridge, and the two stayed on the bridge almost a full half-hour, looking at the reflection of the moon on the water and listening to the soft whooshes from the water mill on the bank. Both stopped talking about Nigel, and the ball, and the fact that they were together, and Salisa didn't know why. Instead, they concentrated on simply absorbing those minutes in Abingdon. The sights, the sounds, the smells. . .the soft glow and noises that floated around them from the several balls that were still going on.

At some point during their stop at Mill Bend Bridge, Salisa felt as if she loved the handsome stranger she was with. Putting the name "Bennett" on the person made her panic, so she pretended he was someone new, an interloper who had stolen her away from the ball to make the rest of her

Abingdon dreams come true. It was still somewhat dark and Salisa thought she would be able to continue her mental games with herself without Bennett noticing.

But Bennett did notice. Salisa was gentler, yet more sparkling in her conversation. She touched him occasionally, apparently on instinct. Wisely, Bennett didn't acknowledge the changes. Instead, he calmly identified several competing bird calls and pointed out a few star constellations that hadn't dissolved in the summer-solstice dawn. Abingdon was awakening, and neither of them wanted to ruin the magic of the moment.

"I have something else to show you," said Bennett. "But we have to hurry if we're going to make it there before the sun comes up."

In a burst of abandon, Salisa took off her red heels. Her nylons would be shot, but she wanted to see what her handsome escort had planned next. "Let's go," she whispered. She knew where she would have liked to have gone at this moment, but she didn't voice it, afraid that it would only make wherever they were going less special.

Bennett led her up the path on the other side of the riverbank, and up the small side path that ended at Palace Green, the square grassy area that separated the Abingdon's cathedral from its castle. Ancient buildings lined the sides of the green, and Salisa had spent many weekend afternoon teatimes wandering from the cathedral to one of the Green's coffee houses, to the castle, and back to the cathedral.

When they stepped out into the Green, which was still dark because of the surrounding buildings' many shadows, Salisa stopped in awe. The graves in front of the cathedral didn't scare her, but they looked eerier than usual in the soft, hazy light. The entire scene gave Salisa the sense that here was history, and that the place had looked the same at dawn for centuries upon centuries.

"It gets better than this," said Bennett, pulling her

gently again.

"Where else can we go?" asked Salisa. "Everything's locked."

"That's what you think."

Bennett had a key—to the cathedral.

"Where. . .how?" Salisa asked as Bennett began to open a small side door on the west side of the cathedral.

"I worked with one of the vicars when Chadwick had their charity week a few months ago," explained Bennett. "We got to be pretty good friends. I've already cleared this with him, so don't worry." Then he led Salisa through the dark cathedral toward the stairway that led to the bell tower.

"Bennett, are you sure we won't get in trouble?" Salisa whispered.

"Do you want to do this or don't you?" asked Bennett, not stopping to look back at her. Somehow he knew how much she did, so he left it at that.

Salisa had been up the winding, stone, spiral staircase many times before, but never in the dark. Bennett, always prepared, helped her as much as he could with his small flashlight.

Up and up, the stairs became narrower and steeper. Salisa always enjoyed this part of the climb, for just when she thought she could stand the claustrophobia no more, the door to the balcony would appear.

When it did, Bennett pushed it open, and cool, almost cold, air wafted past them. It was fresh, and Salisa gulped it in. Bennett helped her onto the wooden planks that created a path around the top. The middle of the balcony was an encased group of lightning rods.

Salisa waited until she had both feet planted firmly on the planks and both hands on the iron guardrails before she allowed herself to look through one of the foot-wide spaces between the pointy pillars of the tower. She couldn't speak. The rolling hills, with their paths and rows of miniature homes, and the clusters of college buildings that sprouted along the outskirts of town were all tinged with a sparkling, goldish pink. From this height, Salisa could see the sun as it touched the tips of Abingdon. "Is this what heaven will look like?" she asked Bennett.

Bennett was walking away from her, beckoning her to follow. "It gets better over here," he whispered, as if afraid to disturb the silence of the morning. "You'd better take a quick look all around while the sun's still low."

Salisa followed him, stopping to gaze at each view as long as Bennett would let her. In her mind, she traced the paths she walked so often. . .there was St. Anne's, and beyond that were the Botanical Gardens where she liked to sit and read. On the next to last side were vast fields that Salisa wasn't as familiar with, but the final side yielded the best view of all—Palace Green.

As she stood there looking beyond the castle, all the way to the small lights that indicated the Chadwick ball was still going on, Bennett came up to stand behind her. He wrapped his strong arms around her, and she felt small and safe as he enveloped her. Salisa could feel him relax and she let him dip his head in behind hers. She returned the gesture by reaching back and around to kiss him lightly on the ear.

She saw him open his eyes. "Why'd you do that, Salisa?"

"Because I wanted to."

"Why did you want to?"

Salisa returned to her view of Palace Green. "I've. . .I've always wanted to, I guess," she said. "But I'm still not sure why I want to."

Bennett chuckled at Salisa's incoherence. "Why do you need to know why you want to?" he prodded gently.

Salisa had a ready answer. "Because then I'll know if what I'm feeling is real or not," she said plainly, as if this was a truth everybody should know. Her sensibilities returning, Salisa banished the dreamgirl that had inhabited her body for the past half-hour or so.

"Sweet Salisa," he said, turning her around to face him. "I won't say that I figured it out before you did because that will make you angry, and you'll go stomping off like you've done before. But think for a moment about who you are. Who I am. Put some of the pieces together. Think about how much we've learned together. . .both here and at home. Think about all the fun we've shared, and how it feels when we're together." Bennett let these words sink in.

"But you and I don't go together," Salisa offered, again in her matter-of-fact tone. "We're both Americans, and you're very handsome, but you need the Hazel type. Maybe not Hazel herself, but someone like her who can maintain your city life. And I need someone with a real mission in life. I like the missionary and minister type. I thought you knew that."

Salisa realized that her words might sound callous, but she was trying to be honest and kind all at the same time. She studied Bennett's expression, afraid to see that she had hurt him.

But he was still smiling a peaceful smile. "Why do you think people like Nigel and Dale are the only ones with a real mission in life?" Bennett asked gently.

Salisa thought for a moment, and then said, "With Nigel, that's all there is. That's why it seems so strong. Even though he can be a bit boring sometimes, he's still very stable and secure. And spiritual. Dale was the same way. People like that *seem* boring because the important things they think about take up so much time." Salisa was glad Bennett was asking her all these questions. They were helping her solidify the facts that sometimes didn't always seem so certain in her own mind. Talking them over with Bennett was helping her stay clear-headed.

"So Nigel's the ninety-five percent mission type with about five percent left over for other things."

"Exactly!" said Salisa, happy that Bennett was being so articulate.

"That's very noble," Bennett acknowledged.

"Very," Salisa agreed.

"But did you ever stop to realize," began Bennett, "that there are some people who are ninety-five percent mission and ninety-five percent zest for all the other wonderful things God has put into their lives?" Before Salisa could answer, Bennett said quickly, "I think you're that kind of person, Salisa." And without him saying it, Salisa knew that Bennett was, too.

"So it doesn't have to be one or the other?" Salisa asked, really only looking for confirmation of what Bennett had already pointed out.

"I think you're the one who made up that restriction," said Bennett gently. "Why don't you try to give God credit for *everything* He's put into people, not just their spirituality? He's a God of diversity and creativity, not just single-minded seriousness."

The truth sank in slowly. Bennett was right: she didn't need to feel guilty that she didn't express herself in the same ways Nigel did. And didn't she love Sophie because of her free-for-all personality? Salisa stepped backward for a moment, deep in thought. Her entire view of the world had just been altered, and she needed some time to get her bearings.

But Bennett didn't give her that time. He led her back down the staircase, out the cathedral, and across a few grassy fields, and into the Botanical Gardens. He led Salisa down a few side paths that she hadn't been down before and toward a small clearing that was surrounded by vines and rose bushes. He motioned for her to sit on a small cast-iron bench. A sweet aroma floated all around her as the warmth of the sun began to fill in the shadows and evaporate the dew on the flowers. She watched as Bennett pulled a small book out of his jacket pocket. "I have something to read to you," he said eagerly. Salisa heard the pages rustle as Bennett looked through them, seemingly in a hurry.

Salisa waited. She felt like she was part of an audience, as she had been the night before, anticipating the beginning of Sophie's play.

"The object and the pleasure of mine eye," began Bennett, reading with great flourish of hand movements, "is only Salisa."

Salisa recognized the line from *A Midsummer Night's Dream*, only Bennett had substituted her name for Helena, one of the heroines. Salisa clapped with delight at Bennett's effort to read Shakespeare correctly.

Bennett had stopped, waiting for more of a reaction from Salisa. "I frown upon him, yet he loves me still," Salisa quickly quoted. The words were Hermia's, another character in the play. Salisa was smiling widely, waiting for Bennett to continue. He was flipping back and forth among a few marked pages, looking for an appropriate response. Salisa could tell the precise moment he found the one he was looking for.

"Oh Salisa,. . . nymph, perfect, divine!
To what, my love, shall I compare thine eyne?"

At this point, Bennett looked at Salisa and laughed. "What's an 'eyne'?" Salisa was laughing too hard to respond, so Bennett continued.

"Crystal is muddy! O, how ripe in show
Thy lips, those kissing cherries, tempting grow!
That pure congealed white, high Taurus' snow,
Fanned with the eastern wind, turns to a crow. . . ."

Here Bennett added more commentary. "Is Shakespeare trying to say her face is white and her hair is dark?" When Salisa nodded, Bennett said, "Well, then, why doesn't he just say so?" Then, he continued:

"When thou hold'st up thy hand. O,let me kiss

This princess of pure white, this seal of bliss!"

As he came toward Salisa with his hand dramatically placed on his heart, Salisa held him at arm's length and turned her head. "I give him curses, yet he gives me love." This was another one of Hermia's lines, and Salisa was delighted at how appropriately it fit into the drama she and Bennett were acting impromptu. She was still smiling, waiting to see what Bennett would do next.

Instead of letting her keep him away, he kissed her hand and then firmly folded her arm. Salisa let him come close. They were now staring eye-to-eye, during dawn in the Botanical Gardens, and Salisa could hardly stand the romance of the moment. She searched her mind frantically for some thought that would bring her back to reality, back to that ninety-five percent sensibility she had previously admired.

"You got all these ideas from that Chadwick student that came to me yesterday, didn't you?" Salisa suddenly conjectured. For the last several hours, Salisa had subconsciously wondered how Bennett had become so good at guessing her thoughts. Finally, the face of that persistent student had popped into her mind. And she had given him the perfect script for a perfect evening, complete with romantic allusions to her now-favorite Shakespearean play.

"How now, my love! Why is your cheek so pale?"

Had Salisa had her wits about her just then, she would have been shocked to see that Bennett had recalled this line without even consulting his text. But her mind was somewhere else. And it was true—her face was pale. Since she knew the play backward and forward, she knew what Bennett was about to quote next.

"Will you let me say it then?" he asked. His confident smile and loving eyes dissolved all her fears. She nodded.

Again, without consulting his text, Bennett said:

"O, take the sense of my innocence!

> Love takes the meaning in love's conference;
> I mean that my heart unto yours is knit,
> So that but one heart we can make of it:
> Two hearts interchained with an oath,
> So then two hearts and a single truth.
> Then by your side, no love deny,
> For in loving you, Salisa, I do not lie."

Bennett had adapted this passage somewhat, but Salisa didn't care. She threw her arms around Bennett and started crying. "Yes, Bennett. Yes."

He pushed her back in front of him, took her face in his hands, and wiped the tears away with his thumbs. "You understand what I was saying, then?"

Salisa laughed through her sobs. "Of course, silly! I've studied this play the whole year! Yes!" she repeated. "I want to marry you, too!"

The relief on Bennett's face was evident. He let Salisa return her head to his shoulder and continue crying. "It's all just so romantic and wonderful," she popped her head up long enough to say. Bennett simply continued to embrace her.

"But if I know you, Sal, you'll have second thoughts about all this once you've had a good long nap and some time to analyze everything that's happened."

"No, I won't," came the muffled reply.

But Bennett just smiled and shook his head. "Trust me," he said. "And I want to make sure you remember me saying this, because it's the fact that I *do* know you. . .and love every bit about you. . .that will finally help you believe that you and I belong together."

# twenty

Bennett's prediction that Salisa would recant after a good nap proved to be accurate. Salisa's perspective on life had changed a lot the night of Chadwick's ball, but the transformation wasn't complete enough for Salisa to abandon all the presuppositions that had guided her decisions for twenty-seven years.

"But don't you remember me telling you that you would feel this way," Bennett pleaded the next day when they met where they had agreed to—Mill Bend Bridge. "You can't just forget everything you said last night, Salisa! We talked about some serious things!"

"I feel somewhat tricked," Salisa said, not looking Bennett in the eye. "You preyed on all the dreams I had here at Abingdon. And all the romantic spots you knew I wanted to visit on a romantic summer night. As a result, I wasn't thinking rationally."

"But that's what love sometimes is, Salisa," said Bennett, exasperated. "I put a lot of thought into how I would tell you that yes, I really love you! Ever since I came back from Christmas vacation and sat and listened to your stories about Russia and Europe, and as I watched you interact with people and laugh and pray with them, I've fallen in love with you! And I've done everything I can possibly think of to communicate that to you."

Though Bennett had expected this kind of difficulty from Salisa, she could see that her mixed-up emotions were starting to wear him out. But she still couldn't bring herself to be as vulnerable as she had been the night before. The truth was, she was petrified. She had planned and allowed for every possible end to her year except this one.

Bennett looked angry as he leaned over the stone side of Mill Bend Bridge. Salisa looked up into the blue sky with its drifting white clouds, the same sky she had watched being born that morning.

*I know I asked for a clear sign, God,* she directed upwards. *But this one is just too full of emotion for me to take seriously. A wonderful man makes all my dreams come true, and I'm supposed to believe that this is for real?* She looked over at Bennett who, for the first time Salisa could remember, didn't look calm or peaceful about what was happening.

"Bennett," Salisa said evenly. "I've thought about this a lot this morning—"

"Give it more time, then!" interrupted Bennett.

"You seem to think a romantic night, shadows, and an extremely late hour constitute good decision-making conditions, so why can't something decided in a clear-headed morning be even better?"

Bennett didn't have a response.

Another objection that had come to Salisa that morning was that Bennett had seemed to expect her to return home with him. They hadn't decided on any specifics of the future, only that they wanted to be together. As far as Salisa knew, Bennett had no idea that she had made definite plans to stay. In fact, Salisa hadn't even known anything definite until that morning.

She had run over to Wiltshire Hall to discuss some of the options Maureen had given her, one of which was staying on at St. Anne's another year. That was the one Salisa had suddenly decided she would take. She wasn't ready to go with Nigel and Sophie to Asia, and she didn't want to return to Pepperton, especially after what had transpired with both Dale *and* Bennett. The choice, then, seemed fairly clear. She'd keep her room at St. Anne's and find a summer job, maybe returning home for a few weeks before the fall term began.

Salisa felt guilty hiding all these plans from the man she had professed to love only a few hours before. He had planned so hard! *But he preyed on my emotions, too*, Salisa reminded herself. That thought toughened her. Somehow she had to get through this last interchange with Bennett, and then she would be free to think about a fresh start next year. Things had gotten more mixed up than she could have ever imagined.

"Bennett," Salisa lightly put her hand on his arm. He continued to stare out over the river, letting the breeze slightly move his thick waves. "We can't pretend that what we've experienced over here is reality. We need to go back to what it was like before. Friends. Even acquaintances.

"You need to concentrate on finishing up your residency," Salisa continued. She had rehearsed her points carefully. "And so many of your relatives live and work together in Lansing . . .won't they expect you to be the same Bennett Havana they said goodbye to last fall?" And though she didn't say it, Salisa suspected that Hazel and Bennett would reunite if left alone to do so. What if she went home engaged to Bennett, and *he* was the one who wanted to back out of the relationship once the spell of Abingdon wore off? No thanks, Salisa didn't want to risk that. Staying in Abingdon another year would give her more time. Then, if she returned, both Bennett and Dale would probably be comfortably settled into their own lives, possibly with partners.

"It can't work," Salisa repeated, hoping Bennett would say *something* now that she had said what she had planned to say.

"You're the one putting the 'can't' on it, Salisa," Bennett said sadly. But he was determined not to beg and not to argue. His perseverance shattered, Salisa could tell that he had given up. She almost ran after him when he turned his back and walked away slowly. But her pride kept her feet planted firmly on the ground. She felt safe but very, very lonely.

A week or so later, there was a knock on Salisa's door at St. Anne's. She was finishing some writing assignments from Maureen who had asked her to help put together a brochure for next year's American students.

"Who is it?" Salisa called.

"Bennett," was the reply.

Salisa slowly opened the door. Bennett didn't look like his usual happy self, but his calm confidence had returned.

"I thought you had already gone home by now," Salisa said, not even inviting him in. She wanted to spare what emotions both of them had left and not get into any heavy discussions. "Didn't you have an evening flight the day after Chadwick's ball?"

"I did," said Bennett. "I went home for a week. But what we didn't get a chance to talk about before you backed out of the proposal was the fact that I'll be here for most of the summer. I have an internship at the Abingdon Infirmary, then I'll go home for a few weeks before the first term starts up again in October."

Salisa's mouth was hanging open. "You mean you're coming back?"

Bennett nodded. "I'm staying another year, Salisa. So don't worry about what we'll have to do when we return to—how did you phrase it—'the reality of home.' You won't have to worry about avoiding me because I won't be there."

"But you can't stay," Salisa said blankly, almost without emotion.

"Why not?"

"Because I am."

After a few seconds' worth of silence while both realized that they had chosen the same path in an effort to avoid each other, Bennett was the first to speak.

"Well, then, I have plenty of time to talk some sense into you."

Salisa mirrored Bennett as his face broke into a smile. "I

don't think it will take that long," she said softly, trying to choke back her rising emotion.

"As for now, though," Bennett said slyly as he began backing out of the doorway, "I'll just let you be by yourself," He was quickly learning how to handle Salisa's roller-coaster emotions. "You seem to need some time to pull yourself together."

"No! No!" Salisa cried and laughed at the same time. "Don't leave me right now. Can you come in and just sit with me for a while?" Suddenly, pride took a back seat. Salisa wanted to be with Bennett, and she didn't care how she communicated that to him. "How about a cup of tea?" she asked. Bennett was staring at her eager expression as if trying to cement in his memory forever the look on her face.

Instead of voicing an acceptance to Salisa's invitation, Bennett drew her toward him and let her nuzzle up to his chest. "My silly, sweet Salisa," he murmured softly. "I'll learn how to figure you out yet."

"Good," said Salisa, pushing herself away from his embrace, "because I can't figure myself out!" Then she returned to that hard yet comfortable chest and buried her head under his chin. A few sniffles escaped.

"Salisa," Bennett jokingly reprimanded, "are you crying again?"

"Don't you know me well enough yet to know that this is how I express happiness?" Salisa looked up and smiled as she cried.

"Then go ahead and cry all you want," said Bennett.

But Salisa decided she would rather kiss Bennett. So he let her. And the kisses he returned promised years of love and passion and fun to come.

•

# *A Letter To Our Readers*

Dear Reader:

In order that we might better contribute to your reading enjoyment, we would appreciate your taking a few minutes to respond to the following questions. When completed, please return to the following:

Rebecca Germany, Editor
Heartsong Presents
P.O. Box 719
Uhrichsville, Ohio 44683

1. Did you enjoy reading *Midsummer's Dream*?
   ☐ Very much. I would like to see more books
      by this author!
   ☐ Moderately
      I would have enjoyed it more if _____

   _____

2. Are you a member of *Heartsong Presents*? Yes   No
   If no, where did you purchase this book? _____

   _____

3. What influenced your decision to purchase
   this book? (Circle those that apply.)

   | | |
   |---|---|
   | Cover | Back cover copy |
   | Title | Friends |
   | Publicity | Other _____ |

4. On a scale from 1 (poor) to 10 (superior), please rate the following elements.

___Heroine     ___Plot

___Hero     ___Inspirational theme

___Setting     ___Secondary characters

5. What settings would you like to see covered in *Heartsong Presents* books?

_____

_____

6. What are some inspirational themes you would like to see treated in future books?_____

_____

_____

7. Would you be interested in reading other *Heartsong Presents* titles?     Yes     No

8. Please circle your age range:

| | | |
|---|---|---|
| Under 18 | 18-24 | 25-34 |
| 35-45 | 46-55 | Over 55 |

9. How many hours per week do you read? _____

Name _____

Occupation _____

Address _____

City _____ State _____ Zip _____

# ·········Presents·········

## Great Inspirational Romance at a Great Price!

Heartsong Presents books are inspirational romances in contemporary and historical settings, designed to give you an enjoyable, spirit-lifting reading experience. You can choose from 76 wonderfully written titles from some of today's best authors like Colleen L. Reece, Brenda Bancroft, Janelle Jamison, and many others.

*When ordering quantities less than twelve, above titles are $2.95 each.*

---

SEND TO: Heartsong Presents Reader's Service
P.O. Box 719, Uhrichsville, Ohio 44683

Please send me the items checked above. I am enclosing $_____ (please add $1.00 to cover postage per order. OH add 6.5% tax. PA and NJ add 6%.). Send check or money order, no cash or C.O.D.s, please.
To place a credit card order, call 1-800-847-8270.

NAME _____

ADDRESS _____

CITY/STATE_____ZIP _____

HPS MAY

# LOVE A GREAT LOVE STORY?
## Introducing Heartsong Presents —
### Your Inspirational Book Club

Heartsong Presents Christian romance reader's service will provide you with four never before published romance titles every month! In fact, your books will be mailed to you at the same time advance copies are sent to book reviewers. You'll preview each of these new and unabridged books before they are released to the general public.

These books are filled with the kind of stories you have been longing for—stories of courtship, chivalry, honor, and virtue. Strong characters and riveting plot lines will make you want to read on and on. Romance is not dead, and each of these romantic tales will remind you that Christian faith is still the vital ingredient in an intimate relationship filled with true love and honest devotion.

Sign up today to receive your first set. Send no money now. We'll bill you only $9.97 post-paid with your shipment. Then every month you'll automatically receive the latest four "hot off the press" titles for the same low post-paid price of $9.97. That's a savings of 50% off the $4.95 cover price. When you consider the exaggerated shipping charges of other book clubs, your savings are even greater!

**THERE IS NO RISK**—you may cancel at any time without obligation. And if you aren't completely satisfied with any selection, return it for an immediate refund.

**TO JOIN**, just complete the coupon below, mail it today, and get ready for hours of wholesome entertainment.

Now you can curl up, relax, and enjoy some great reading full of the warmhearted spirit of romance.

┌ ── ── ──  **Curl up with Heartsong!** ── ── ── ┐

# YES! Sign me up for Heartsong!

**NEW MEMBERSHIPS WILL BE SHIPPED IMMEDIATELY!**
Send no money now. We'll bill you only $9.97 post-paid with your first shipment of four books. Or for faster action, call toll free 1-800-847-8270.

NAME _____

ADDRESS _____

CITY _____ STATE / ZIP _____
MAIL TO: HEARTSONG / P.O. Box 719 Uhrichsville, Ohio 44683
YES II